CHRISTIAN McKAY

WITH ILLUSTRATIONS

SCARY STORIES for YOUNG FOXES

THORNDIKE PRESS
A part of Gale, a Cengage Company

GALE
A Cengage Company

**LIBRARY OF CONGRESS CIP DATA ON FILE.
CATALOGUING IN PUBLICATION FOR THIS BOOK
IS AVAILABLE FROM THE LIBRARY OF CONGRESS.**

ISBN-13: 978-1-4328-8235-8 (hardcover alk. paper)

Published in 2020 by arrangement with Henry Holt and Company.

Printed in Mexico
Print Number: 06   Print Year: 2021

CONTENTS

1. Miss Vix 15
2. Six Sisters 51
3. House of Trix 99
4. Creeeaaak THUMP! Creeeaaak
   THUMP! 173
5. The Slither Out of Darkness . .207
6. The Lilac Kingdom 251
7. The Paw 309
8. The Snow Ghost. 343

THE HAUNTED SEASON had arrived in the Antler Wood.

The sky grayed, the leaves blushed red, and mist coiled through the trees like something alive. Even the pumpkins began to rot and show their true faces.

On these chilled autumn nights, it was best for fox kits to remain near their den on the edge of the wood. There, they could feast on apples that tumbled from high branches. They could hunt for smoky acorns and crunchy stick bugs and juicy mice. And when dusk turned to starlight, the kits could return to their den, tuck under their mother's fur, and be soothed by her heartbeat.

"Tell us a story," the alpha kit said one misty night.

"Make it scary!" the fourth said, yipping and hopping.

"Yeah!" said the third, snarling. "So scary our eyes fall out of our *heads*."

"Please stop biting my face, children," their mother said.

The kits behaved themselves while she smoothed out a bed for the night.

"Let's see," she said. "How about ... 'Rattlebones'?"

"*Mo-om!*" the beta said, rolling her eyes.

"You told us that story when we were *two weeks*," said the alpha.

"It's *boring!*" said the fourth.

"Very well ..." Their mom began ripping out roots that had snuck through the den's walls. "How about 'Willoughby Wallaby and the Floating Paw'?"

"*Seriously?*" the fifth kit said.

"That story wouldn't raise the hackles on a field mouse!" said the fourth.

"It's *kit* stuff," said the third.

"Well," their mom said. "Those are the stories I know."

Seven little foxes sighed.

"Sorry to be a disappointment," their mom said, lying down. She paused and looked at the kits with all seriousness. "But you must promise that no matter what you do tonight, you will not go to Bog Cavern."

The kits' ears perked.

"What's ... Bog Cavern?" the alpha asked.

"That's where the old storyteller lives," their mom said. "If you go there, you'll hear a story so frightening it will put the white in your tail."

The kits stared at their thin, dusty brown tails with wide eyes.

"Wait a second," the fourth said, looking at the fluffy white end of their mom's tail. "*You* heard the story?"

"Only part," she answered. "And I wouldn't repeat what I heard for a thousand mice."

The kits gave one another meaningful looks. They didn't want some toothless story like "Willoughby Wallaby," which could be forgotten with a shiver and some milk and a lick on the cheek. They wanted a story so scary it would prove their bravery and change them forever.

All except the little one, that was. She preferred the sound of her mom's heartbeat.

Yes, it may have been wise for fox kits to stay close to the den once the leaves began to fall. But the fog and the frost and the old crimson moon had stirred something in their whiskers. And so they waited till all was quiet, save their mother's snoozing.

And then seven little foxes slipped out of their den with a mission to scare some white into their tails.

Seven kits snuck into the night — over the log, around the stone, across the creek, and through the grass ... deep into the Antler Wood.

The trees threw up their limbs as if to frighten them away.

The little one slowed at their warning.

"C'mon, sticky paws!" the beta kit whispered.

Seven kits crept through the wood — beneath the bone-white branches, past the broken trap, beyond the cave of snoring, over the human bones ... to the entrance of Bog Cavern.

Roots dripped over its mouth. Fog oozed from its throat. The kits squinted into the darkness but saw nothing but a pile of bones and skin.

"Is the storyteller ... *dead*?" the fifth kit whispered.

The fourth kit sniffed. *Snff snff.* "Doesn't smell dead."

"Someone go nose it awake!" the third kit said.

"Don't look at me!" said the beta. "I *like* my nose."

"*Shh!*" said the alpha.

The bones stirred, then jerked up so abruptly every one of the kits' paws left the ground. The little one scurried behind her beta sister.

The bones sat themselves upright, forming a sort of fox silhouette. Eyes flashed green in the darkness.

"*What have we here?*" the storyteller said with a voice like spilling dust. *Snff. Snfffff.* "Hmph. Grovelers."

The beta gave the alpha a nudge.

"Oh, um," the alpha said, voice cracking. "Would you tell us a scary story, uh, please?"

The storyteller sniffed again. "Too young. Come back when you've lost your milk teeth."

The fox kits clamped their muzzles shut. The little one hoped this was enough to get her siblings to scurry home, but no one budged.

The alpha cleared his throat and delivered the speech he'd prepared. "We're, um, smart enough to know that stories are as harmless as the wind through the leaves. They cannot pluck our whiskers or break our bones or, um, strip our skins."

A silence grew behind the roots, so complete it seemed it could suck the kits into the darkness.

"Sure of that, are you?" the storyteller asked.

Seven little foxes tried not to shiver. Two of them succeeded.

"All scary stories have two sides," the storyteller said. "Like the bright and dark of the moon. If you're brave enough to listen and wise enough to stay to the end, the stories can shine a light on the good in the world. They can guide your muzzles. They can help you survive."

A cloud slid off the moon, and shadows reared up around the cavern. The Antler Wood seemed darker now that there was light.

"*But*," the storyteller said, "if you don't listen closely … if you turn tail from the horror and don't stay till the end, then the darkness of the story can swallow all hope.

It can frighten you so deeply you'll never want to leave your den again. You'll waste away the days with your mother, forever smelling like her milk."

The wind pawed at the leaves. The moon shined on the gray fur of the storyteller's face.

"So. Do you still want to hear a scary story?"

Seven little foxes gulped. Only the alpha nodded.

"Come closer, then," the storyteller said. "And we'll see which of you makes it to the end."

The alpha marched forward. The third hesitated a moment and then followed. Then came the beta and the fourth, fifth, and sixth, trembling.

The littlest fox gazed back through the Antler Wood — over the bones, beyond the cave, past the trap, beneath the branches, through the grass, across the creek, around the stone, over the log — toward home. She breathed deep and padded close to the cavern with her siblings.

Seven little foxes sat and listened.

"Our story begins," the storyteller said, "in the Eavey Wood …"

MISS
VIX

ONE

The sun was only just peeking over the peachleaf trees, but the heat was already crisping the leaves and steaming the creek and making the dying fields too bright to look at.

Roa, Marley, and Mia trotted toward the dappled shade of the Eavey Wood, tongues lolling. The grasses buzzed deliciously around them, but on these high-sun days, the grasshoppers were as dry and sour as birch bark.

"Whaddaya think we'll learn today?" Roa said.

"Hopefully about shadows and holes and how to take *naps* in them," said Mia, panting.

Marley was busy rolling in something smelly and didn't hear the question.

"Come on, Mar," Roa said. "We're gonna be late."

Every morning, when the sky woke white and watery, when the owls were tucking into their trunks and the snakes had not warmed up yet, the kits gathered beneath the Learning Tree for their lessons. Their teacher was called Miss Vix, and she taught them what they needed to know while their mother tended to the hunting and the den.

In their first few weeks outside the den, Miss Vix had taught the kits how to swish their tails through the reeds to stir up a buzzy explosion of insects, which they could snap out of the air. She taught them how to point their muzzles northward when hunting, waiting for the claw of the Sky Fox to draw a hazy ring of purple around their prey.

She taught them the birdsong for "eagle" and "snake," so they knew whether to duck or jump when a predator was near. And when there were no birds in the treetops to sound the alarm, Miss Vix taught them how to perk their ears and listen for the sounds of large feathers brushing the wind or golden scales parting the earth.

Months from now, after the breath of autumn blew red into the leaves, the kits would celebrate their Golden-Eyed Day, and they would set out to claim their own territories. But until that day came, they would learn how to become proper foxes.

Something flopped fatly across the three kits' path.

Roa sniffed the creature's damp skin and pond breath, and gagged. "*Blech.* Toad slime."

"Catcher gets belly!" Marley said, hips in a wiggle.

Mia collapsed in the shade of a wilting rosebush. "Too hot."

Marley bounded after the toad while Roa gazed toward the Learning Tree and sighed.

"Don't *worry*," Mia said, fixing him with her blue-swirl eyes. "Miss Vix won't get any less pretty, and your eyes won't get any less *blue*."

Roa scowled. He tried to think of a comeback, but instead his ear twitched.

This sent Mia into hysterics. "So it's *true!*" She rolled onto her back and addressed him upside down. "You wanna marry Miss Vix and start an *adorable* little den with her!"

He tackled his sister, and they lashed at each other with their milk teeth. But the day's heat quickly made them both give up in a panting puddle.

There came a wet plop in a nearby pond, and Marley came bounding back, shaking mud from his muzzle. "It was too slippery."

"Psh," Mia said, rounding to her paws. "That jumper was as dry as dust." She trotted toward the Learning Tree and called back to Roa. "C'mon, *Mr. Vix!*"

Roa followed, grumbling.

It was true that Miss Vix had honeyed eyes and lush black ears and golden fur that smelled like butterfly dust. And it was true that the tip of her tail was as white as cloud fluff and her boots were as black as the space between the stars.

But Roa didn't want to start a den with her. He wanted to *be* like her when he grew up. He admired the arc in his teacher's back whenever she pounced on her prey ... the way she could sniff out a scuttling from a distance of three hundred tails ... and how she had once stolen a badger's feast, piece by piece, by nipping at the badger's ears and getting it to chase her.

The three siblings continued on, panting. They passed the sluggish river, fish glittering in the sun. They passed the bush with shriveled raspberries that tasted as bright as lightning. And they passed Lumpy Prairie, where cottontail season had finally come to an end. The grass was growing brittle, and baby bunnies were no longer as easy to pluck as blackberries off the vine.

"Melting," Marley said.

"Evaporating," said Mia.

Roa just panted.

No birds sang in the Eavey Wood that morning. The leaves rasped like an old, dying snake.

TWO

After a short, sunbaked trot, Roa, Marley, and Mia leapt atop the tumbled oak that bordered meadow and wood.

"Huh," Mia said, curling her lip. "Does something smell" — *snff snff* — "*funny* to you guys?"

Roa blinked away the shadows left by the sun. He sniffed the trees. Miss Vix's butterfly scent was lost on the wind. It had been replaced with something darker. Something … *yellow*.

Snrrrrrt! Marley snorted thickly. "I don't smell anything."

He bounded off the tumbled oak. Mia and Roa gave each other a look and then followed. The three arrived beneath the shade of the Learning Tree, stopping at the hawthorn bush where Miss Vix greeted them every morning.

22

Their teacher was nowhere in sight.

Bizy, the kits' alpha sister, sat in front of the bush, head tilted. Every morning, when they left the den, she sprinted ahead, like reaching the Learning Tree was some sort of race.

"You win again, Biz!" Marley said, out of breath.

Bizy glanced at them. She didn't brag about her win like she usually did. Instead, she stared back into the hawthorn bush. Its branches were trembling.

Roa sniffed — *snff snff* — and the yellow stench crept up his nostrils and roiled his stomach.

"*Yuck,*" Marley said, pawing at his nose. "What *died* in there?"

"Smells like shrew barf," Mia said, wrinkling her muzzle.

"It's —" Bizy's head tilted to the other side. "It's M-Miss Vix."

Roa's ears perked while his heart made a little jump.

"What the squip is she teaching?" Mia said. "How to stink so bad you scare away all the prey?"

Marley laughed. Roa sniffed at the bush again. Beneath the yellow, he caught a faint scent, dusty sweet and familiar. Bits of golden fur flashed between the shifting leaves. In the shadows, he could barely make out the silhouette of a fox. Its head swayed back and forth like an eel in water. Its mouth hung open as if tasting the air.

"That's not Miss Vix … ," Roa said. "Is it?"

He took a step toward the bush, but then something sharp clamped down on his tail. He whirled and tackled Bizy to the ground. She caught his paw in her teeth.

"Mif Vikff seh don' go in ver," she said.

Roa loosed his paw from her mouth and gave it a lick.

"Maybe it's a game!" Marley said, tail wagging.

"It is!" Mia said. "It's called Who Stinks the Worst." *Snff snff.* "Marley wins!"

He pounced on her, and they rolled away.

Roa hadn't taken his eyes from the swaying silhouette. Beneath the rustle of leaves, he could hear a hair-raising click of teeth — *klik … klik klik.*

"What's she doing in there, Biz?" Roa asked his alpha sister.

Bizy flattened her ears. "When I got here, everything was n-n-normal. Normal day. N-n-normal Miss Vix ..." She swallowed deep and stared into the bush. "Except for Alfie."

Alfie may have been the runt of the litter, but he was the most adventurous. Their mom could never get him to stay put near the den, and she'd given up trying long ago. Alfie would disappear for hours at a time and return smelling of orange mud or hairy leaves and, one time, even bear dung.

"He was hiding in the b-b-bushes," Bizy said, her stutter worse than usual. "A-a-and he smelled *funny*. M-Miss Vix was trying to get him to c-come out. Sh-sh-she kept asking, 'Are you hurt? Are you h-hurt?' When he didn't answer, sh-sh-she grabbed him by his tail and p-pulled him out." Bizy swallowed deep. "Alfie looked ... *d-different*. His fur was all muddy and slicked back. His legs were gn-gnawed pink. All the fur on his tail was g-gone except a little t-tuft at the end. His lips jumped off his t-t-teeth and his breath was fast and s-squeaky. His p-pupils were as wide as the night sky ...”

Bizy whimpered, and Roa cleaned her ears until she was soothed. In the hawthorn bush, the paws of the dark silhouette twitched up off the ground, like they'd stepped in ants.

“Miss Vix went to lick Alfie's w-wounds,” Bizy said, “but h-h-he bit her paw. *Hard.* Then he r-ran off. Miss Vix licked her paw, and I saw b-blood drip.”

She turned her nose to a little black spatter in the dust. Roa stared at it.

“I a-asked if she was okay,” Bizy said, “b-but she just stood there and t-t-trembled. Then she said, ‘C-class is over,’ and crawled into the b-b-bush.”

The silhouette moved its jaws. A breeze made the leaves sharpen themselves against one another. Roa held back a shudder. Had Alfie wandered somewhere and come back smelling of yellow? Had he given the yellow to Miss Vix when he bit her?

“Still playing the stinky game?” Mia asked, returning from her battle with Marley.

Roa stared into the bush. "I'm gonna go in and check on her."

"I d-dunno about that," Bizy said.

"Do it!" Marley said. "I'd do it, but I don't think my butt would fit in there."

Behind the leaves, the silhouette stopped swaying and held perfectly still ... as if listening. Roa hesitated.

"What if it's a test?" Mia said, narrowing her blue-swirl eyes. "We're not supposed to go in strange and stinky places. What if you go in there and Miss Vix bites your scruff and you fail at everything forever?"

Roa rocked paw to paw. "But what if I *don't* go in there and I fail?"

The silhouette seemed to stare at him, as if waiting for an answer.

Roa nodded, determined. "I'm going in."

"Well, you've said that *twice* now," Mia said. "But times you've gone in there? *Zero*."

Roa let out an involuntary whimper. He licked his lips and made a backward wiggle. Then, folding his ears, he plopped to his belly and crawled beneath the leaves.

THREE

It was dark in the hawthorn bush. But then a soft wind blew, flickering the leaves, and patches of light cleaned the shadows from the silhouette.

It was Miss Vix.

Roa had never seen his teacher upset before. She had always taken the kits' bites and scratches with the patience of spring. But here, in the hawthorn bush, her lips were curled around the black of her gums, the whites of her teeth. Her eyes were narrowed in dark, gooey slits.

"Miss Vix?" Roa whispered.

A shudder ran from his teacher's ears straight to the tip of her tail. She tried to take a step toward his voice, but then wavered and missed. She turned in a half circle, then sat down again. Her gooey eyes stared at nothing.

Roa looked at his teacher's paw, sticky with black. "Are you hurt, Miss Vix? Do you want me to find Alfie and bite him for you?"

Miss Vix's head swayed. Her breath sounded choked with cobwebs.

"What's she doing?" Mia whispered from outside the bush.

Roa didn't answer.

"Miss Vix?" he said. "Are you okay?"

Miss Vix lifted her snout. And she saw him through the goo. Her muzzle tightened into a snarl, but then she shook her head back and forth, like she was trying to escape a sneeze.

A sound bubbled from her throat. *"Run."*

Roa's ears flattened. "Run where?"

He had never done anything in the Eavey Wood without his teacher's permission.

Miss Vix's teeth made that horrible clicking. *Klik klik — klik klik.* The sound woke the nerves in Roa's toenails.

"Run *where*, Miss Vix?"

Her breath made a rattling sound. With it came the stench, dark and warm. The scent of butterfly dust was gone. As if the yellow had swallowed his teacher from the inside out.

Roa dropped to his belly and scooted back out of the hawthorn bush.

"Did you pass the test?" Mia asked in a chipper voice. "Are you guys *married* now?"

Her giggles were cut short when there came a snapping of branches and Miss Vix stumbled out of the leaves. The other kits saw their teacher's gooey eyes, her snarled lips, and they backed away, whiskers alert.

Bizy whimpered, lifting her paws. "M-maybe we should go."

"Yeah," Marley said, backing up. "I think I hear Mom calling."

Roa planted his paws. "I'm staying."

Mia's tail thumped uncertainly.

Their teacher stared at them with her black goo eyes. Her teeth dripped.

"Thaaaaaaaat's enough class for me today," Mia said.

She tried to scamper away, but Miss Vix struck like a snake, snagging Mia by the tail. Mia let out a deafening yelp before kicking free of their teacher's teeth and disappearing into the hawthorn bush, where she fell silent.

Bizy whimpered. Marley flopped on his side in submission. Roa froze. Their teacher had never bitten any of them before.

Miss Vix's gooey eyes flashed back to the three kits, Mia's fur sticking out of her fangs. Miss Vix lunged at each of them in turn. Roa. Marley. Bizy. As each kit flinched out of her jaws' reach, the next caught her attention and she rounded on them.

Roa backed away from his teacher, heart thumping. He wanted to stay put. He wanted to sniff out the butterfly dust beneath the yellow and coax her back to the surface ... but his paws betrayed him. He turned his muzzle toward the den and started to pad away.

Behind him, there came a chomp and a tiny yelp. *"Yipe!"*

Bizy. She didn't even get a head start.

Roa broke into a run.

There came a scuffle and another yelp. *"Aroo!"*

Marley. He wasn't laughing anymore.

Roa started to sprint.

31

Three yelps from three of his siblings. The yellow stench had swallowed Miss Vix. Now it would swallow them too.

Roa ran through the dappled shade of the Learning Tree and leapt onto the sun-touched moss of the tumbled oak. In the warm light of morning, he second-guessed himself and gazed back toward the hawthorn bush. There was still a world of things to learn. Miss Vix was going to teach them the nap-and-capture technique. She was going to teach them how to tell if a mouse was playing dead. She was going to teach them how to swim.

The hawthorn bush was hidden by the trunk of the Learning Tree. The only movement was the shifting shadow of the canopy.

"Bizy?" Roa croaked. "Marley? M-Mia?"

His teacher came sprinting around the trunk, fangs bared, drool streaming, gooey eyes fixed on him.

Roa's paws kneaded the moss. "I give up, Miss Vix!"

Still, she came. Her cobwebbed breath. Her bloodied paw. Her yellow stench.

"I fail!" Roa shouted at her. "I don't pass! I ... don't want to do this anymore!"

It wasn't until she leapt from the earth, lips curled, teeth gleaming, that a voice echoed deep in Roa's mind.

"Never the fields," his teacher had said when she still smelled like butterfly dust. *"Your legs are too little to escape a hunter in the open. If something is chasing you, hide yourself in the most tangled space you can. Do you understand?"*

Roa might not have understood, but his paws did. As his teacher's shadow swept over him, he slipped off the back side of the tumbled oak, plopped to the ground, and bolted toward the den faster than he thought possible. He heard the crunch of Miss Vix's paws on the trunk behind him as she landed and then leapt again. When he sensed her shadow in his left whiskers, his legs swiveled and shot him to the right.

Soon, he could feel the *klik klik klik* of her hot breath snapping at his tail as his paws leapt and bounded and skittered through the trees. He tried to think of the most tangled space he knew of.

The briar patch.

The wood was a blurred confusion. Roa couldn't tell which way was which. Then he remembered when Miss Vix taught them how to tell directions.

Whenever you point your muzzle northward, your eyes will grow fuzzy with purple.

Roa swung his head left, then right, until his vision gained a hazy color, like sunset coming in at the edges. He rocketed toward the purple, crossing through Lumpy Prairie, and then arrived at the briar patch. He wriggled into a whisker-wide crevice and crawled to the heart of the thorny shadows.

There he crouched, trying to catch his breath.

Safe . . .

Safe . . .

A snarl.

Roa leapt just as Miss Vix's fangs ripped through the brambles. She thrashed toward him, not even flinching as the thorns tore at her gooey eyes.

Roa wriggled out of the briar patch and ran. His teacher chased him across the grasses where she'd taught them to pierce the soft earth with their muzzles.

She chased him through the tunnel where they'd dug for earthworms. She chased him around the blackberry bushes where they'd plucked dessert, and down Tumble Hill where they'd played Hawks and Hunters.

At the bottom of the hill was a sunken creek. Roa tried to leap to the far side, but his ribs struck the ledge and he flipped backward, splashing into the shallows with a small yelp. Quivering, he slunk out of the mud and pressed into the shadow of the crumbling bank, trying to catch his breath without making too much sound.

"Please be a test," he whispered. "Please, please, please."

Moments passed. Flies droned. A raven cawed.

Roa's eyes darted left and right. If he stayed in the sunken creek, Miss Vix would be able to drop down on him from above. But which direction should he run? Upcreek or down? Something told him one way would lead to freedom; the other, to his teacher.

Roa pricked his whiskers. He couldn't see Miss Vix's shadow on the opposite bank or hear her cobwebbed breath over the trickling water. He couldn't smell the yellow stench over the dead fish in the creek. How would he know which way to go?

"Craw! Craw!"

The black feathers of a raven gleamed on a high branch above. Birds had the best view in the forest. They could tell you when something was coming and from what direction. But bird languages were tough. You had to know which birds sang which songs and then remember the subtle changes in trills for what they meant. Roa wasn't as bad at remembering the songs as Mia, but he was nowhere near as good as Bizy, who seemed to have feathers sprouting out of her ears.

"Craw! Craw!"

"I hope you're saying she's coming from the right," Roa whispered to the bird.

He headed upcreek. Whether Miss Vix had actually taught him something about birds or it was pure luck, Roa would never know. But when he rounded up the lip of the sunken bank, he saw his teacher on the far end, staring into the water, muzzle bleeding from the briars.

Her head lifted slowly. The moment she caught his eye, she bounded over the water and came after him.

Again, Roa ran. He panted in the stifling heat. His heart pounded, ready to burst. If this was a test, how could he pass it once and for all? He needed to find somewhere he could hide where his teacher definitely could not fit.

"There's always the mole burrow," Miss Vix had said. *"It's a tight fit, but if your whiskers can get through, so can you."*

Roa darted south this time, opposite the purple, to the shallow part of the river. He bounded across the slimy stones, each threatening to roll were he not quick enough. He heard no splashing behind him, but he didn't stop leaping until he'd made it to the opposite side. Only then did he dare look back.

Miss Vix skidded to a stop on the bank. Her gooey eyes stared at the river. She tried stepping on the first stone, but the moment her paw touched the water, her body seized and arched backward as if something had snatched her by the muzzle and pulled. Her spine bent so far back she could've bitten her own tail.

Roa shook his head, confused. Miss Vix had never been frightened by water. He wanted to go to her, run his muzzle along her back, make her feel okay again. But fear drove him the rest of the way to the mole burrow.

The entrance was barely a crack, pinched by tree roots. He was quite a bit bigger than the last time their teacher had made him and his siblings enter the burrow, but he tried to squeeze inside anyway. His whiskers bent against the soil. The roots folded his ears. A stone yanked his hair and squished his stomach so tight he almost lost his mouse-and-blackberry breakfast.

He was stuck.

Roa clawed and wriggled, but he couldn't slide any deeper. The stone dug painfully into the top of his hip. His hind legs kicked, and his tail whirled. He was numb with the fear of being bitten. He stopped struggling. He remembered Miss Vix's honeyed eyes, her golden fur — the way they used to be — and then he wriggled and kicked with every bit of him that wanted to pass her test.

The stone crumbled free from the earth, and he slid into darkness. His breath came in sobs. Roots and damp soil cradled him on all sides, close and dark and soothing. His fur prickled in the cool of the underground as his breath quieted and his heartbeat finally slowed.

Safe . . .

Safe . . .

. . .

Roa kept his eyes on the small, craggy entrance. He waited for Miss Vix to stick her snout into the burrow and tell him he'd passed the test. He waited for her to help him squeeze back into the sunlight, where she would lick the mud from his fur and nibble the briars from his tail and tell him he was faster and cleverer than all of his siblings.

The wind whistled outside. With it came a sound. A panting. Breath like a spider's nest. That awful clicking of teeth.

Klik. Klik klik.

Roa assured his pounding heart that Miss Vix couldn't fit inside. She was too big.

Klik klik klik.

His ear twitched. This clicking sounded different than before. The breath was higher-pitched.

Klik klik, klik klik.

He flattened his ears as a snout slid into the craggy entrance, breathing the yellow stench into the burrow. It sniffed.

Snff snff.

Roa's heart went cold. This was not Miss Vix's nose. It was too small. Too dry.

Snff snff snfffff.

The fur on the muzzle was muddy and slick ...

Snfffff

"A-Alfie?" Roa said.

The runt looked terrible. His paws were gnawed bloody. His tongue, now black, dangled between his teeth. And his neck twitched like a broken branch in the wind.

Roa pressed his back against the earthen wall. There was no exit. No escape. What had felt close and safe was now much too tight as Alfie wheezed and wriggled his small, ravaged body into the burrow. The last thing Roa saw was his own reflection in his brother's black eyes — as wide and unseeing as a starless sky.

FOUR

On the far side of the Eavey Wood, a small fox arrived back at her den, panting.

"Mama! *Mama!*"

A mother fox stepped into the light. "Mia? Where are your brothers and sister?" She sniffed. "What's wrong? You're — you're *bleeding!*"

Mia caught her breath and then started to cry. "I *ran*, Mama. I ran away."

"Hush, hush," her mom said. "Catch your breath."

Mia didn't wait for her breath to catch. She told her mom the story. She told her how Miss Vix had lashed out and bitten Marley and Bizy and then chased after Roa. She told her about the yellow stench.

Something in her mom's eyes changed.

"What are we waiting for?" Mia asked, her paws itching to go back the way she'd come. "We have to help them!"

42

When her mom didn't move, Mia opened her mouth to drag her toward the Learning Tree ... but her mom stepped away.

"Mia." Her mom's voice trembled. "How did you hurt your tail?"

Mia sniffed at the blood scabbing at her tail's tip. "Miss Vix tried to bite it."

"Mia ..." Her mom kept her distance. "Think carefully. Did Miss Vix bite your skin?"

"I — I don't think so," Mia said. All she wanted was her mom to lick her tail better. "She ... she just pulled out some of the hairs, I think."

Her mother looked lost for a moment. Then determined. "Come, Mia."

Confused, Mia trotted after her, over the leafy roof of their den and past the sandy loam to the nearby sipping creek.

"Drink," her mom said.

"But *Mama*." Mia's paws wouldn't hold still. "Roa ... He's in trouble. Marley. Bizy. They're —"

"*Drink*, I said."

Confused, Mia dipped her muzzle into the creek and took a small lap. The

43

water was cool and clean on her tongue. She hadn't realized how thirsty she was. While she drank long and deep, her mom crouched on the bank, watching Mia's mouth as if she expected the water to leap out of it. When Mia swallowed, her mom gave a deep sigh and trotted away from the den.

Mia licked the droplets from her beard. "Where are you going? Roa. Bizy. Marley. Alfie ... They're *that* way."

Her mom turned her eyes to the edge of the field, to the shadows of the Learning Tree. "We must leave them."

She bounded up Jackrabbit Slope, and Mia practically tripped over her own paws trying to catch up. "But ... where? Why?"

"To the north," her mom said. "Beyond the forest. Where the yellow cannot follow."

"But, *Mama*." Mia sniffed, too exhausted to cry. "We have to go back. I *left* them."

Her mom continued on, ducking beneath the drooping leaves of a willow and slipping into a thicket of ivy. "We don't need to worry about your brothers and sister now ..." She sniffed once. "Miss Vix will take care of them."

44

Mia gazed back down the slope. She traced the sipping creek as it curled into the river, which flowed past the Learning Tree. The shadows seemed darker now — the bright spots gray with rising dust. Almost like the Eavey Wood — her home — was going to sleep.

"Was the yellow stuff ... ," Mia said. "Was it all a test?"

Her mom leapt down the other side of Jackrabbit.

"Yes," she said. "It was a test ... and you passed. The other kits still have learning to do. But you ..." She glanced at Mia with shining eyes. "You're all grown up now."

"Really?" Mia said, following. She struggled to untangle a knot of ivy with her snout. "I don't feel grown up."

"Well ... you are," her mom said, and with a snip of her jaws, she set Mia free. "You did so well in your classes that it's time for you to leave the Eavey Wood."

Her mom continued downhill at a faster pace. But Mia stopped and quirked her head toward the treetops. Her mom had told her that she would celebrate her Golden-Eyed Day after the leaves fell. And that only then would she and her siblings set out on their own.

But there were the leaves, still fluttering on the branches.

"But, Mama," Mia began.

"Hurry now," her mom said.

Mia bounded to catch up. "You'll be with me? The whole time?"

"Every step of the way."

"Okay," Mia said, walking a little more easily now. "That's good."

The world opened before them, new and wide and unfamiliar. And although Mia's paws still trembled, she tried to walk like a fox whose tail didn't sting and who wasn't afraid of the things she'd seen. Mia followed her mom's sweet apple scent, and she tried to pretend she was more grown-up than her pounding heart would let her believe.

THE BRANCHES OF the Antler Wood creaked in a soft wind.

"That's the scariest part, right?" the beta asked. "That's as bad as it gets?"

The storyteller remained silent in the cavern.

"That wasn't *that* scary," the third kit said.

"Are you kidding?" said the fifth. He counted on his toes. "One, two, three, four, *five* foxes died!"

The fourth cleared his throat. "The yellow stench isn't real ... right?"

More silence from the cavern. The fourth kneaded his paws and whimpered.

"Did Mia and her mom ever find another den?" the fifth asked.

"Patience," the storyteller whispered.

The fourth's ear twitched with realization. "Oh, right! *Mia!* That's —"

"Hush," the beta said.

The little one curled her paws beneath her chest to keep them from shaking.

"Uh, Boz?" said the alpha.

Bozy, the sixth kit, hadn't blinked since the story ended. The littlest kit tried to see into her brother's eyes, but they stared straight through her into the dark of the wood.

"Bozy?" the beta said. "Do you need to go home?"

Without a word, the sixth kit stood, turned his nose toward the den, and left.

Six little foxes.

"We're ready for the next part," the alpha said.

"Yeah," said the third. "We're ready for the *scary* part."

The little one gulped, hoping the scary part was over and done with.

"What's more frightening than a rabid teacher?" the storyteller asked.

The kits tilted their heads questioningly, ears still flat.

"Perhaps," the storyteller continued, "someone in your family who is just as cruel, even though they are not diseased."

The wind made the leaves whisper, ruffling the little one's fur. She didn't like where this was going.

"On the other side of the forest lay the Boulder Fields," the storyteller said. "One night, the moon shined high and bright, just like it is now …"

Six little foxes gazed into the sky.

SIX
SISTERS

ONE

"Girls, clean your brother, please."

"*Mo-om,*" Ava said.

"He's *gross,*" said Anna.

"His fur tastes funny," said Ali.

"Like *shrew* guts," Aya said.

"Yeah," Ada and Agatha said together, "and owl pellets."

The sisters' giggles echoed off the walls of the stone den.

Uly, their only brother, listened from a dark corner, wobbling on his one good foreleg. His other leg, the front left one, curled against his chest like a dried-up dandelion stem, the paw a wilting flower. It didn't show any signs of growing like the other three — as much as his mother licked at it.

"*Girls,*" their mother scolded. "Clean your brother now or I'll bite your lips."

Ava huffed, and her huff was echoed five times.

Uly had tried cleaning himself. He really had. But it was impossible to sit upright and run his one good forepaw over his ears without thumping over and bruising his chest. He had tried lying on his side, licking his good forepaw, and swiping at his face. But he always ended up tumbling himself in circles, making his fur even dirtier than before.

"Mom says we have to clean you," Ava said.

"Yeah, so you don't stink up the den," said Anna.

"And attract every hawk in the universe," Ali said.

"And —"

"I *heard*," Uly said before they could continue.

He slid his forepaw forward, slumping to his stomach, and lay his muzzle on the stone. His sisters took little licks at his fur, making it stand out at all angles. Two of them made gagging sounds. Another gave him painful nips instead of licks. Uly knew this was Ava.

54

"I'm going hunting, kits!" their mother called from the den's entrance. "Howl if you see any shadows."

Uly's stomach ached in anticipation of dinner. He wasn't much of a fighter. And because he had to wrestle his six sisters for every morsel of food their mom dragged into the den, he barely ate enough to keep his good legs steady, let alone the shriveled one.

The kits' father was meant to bring fresh kills to the den for their first ten weeks. But Uly's mom told them that their dad had died in a terrible accident before they were born. (And, *no*, she wouldn't say what happened until they were older.) Whatever their mom could hunt and whatever they managed to wrestle from their siblings was what they got to eat.

The moment their mother's shadow vanished up the stone slope, Uly's sisters stopped cleaning, leaving his skin grimy and itchy.

Ava smiled at him. "We won't have to clean you much longer, you know."

"Not much longer now," Ali said.

"Wanna know how we know?" Aya asked.

"No," Uly said in a slump.

"Mr. *Scratch* told us," said Anna.

Uly's jaw clenched. "There's no such thing as Mr. Scratch," he said, even though the name never failed to send a chill to the tip of his tail.

"Oh, Mr. Scratch is real, all right," Ava said.

"As real as *moonlight*," said Aya.

Uly struggled to sit up. "That doesn't even make sense."

Few things about Mr. Scratch made sense. What was he? Where did he come from? And when would his sisters have heard about something Uly hadn't? Had they slipped out of the den at night when he and his mom were asleep? Had they whispered to Mr. Scratch under the light of the moon? The thought gave Uly a case of the moth flutters.

As if smelling his fear, his six sisters started to walk circles around him.

"Mr. Scratch is made of ash."

"Mr. Scratch has teeth that gnash."

"Gobbles all the litters' runts."

"Tiny kits are what he hunts."

"Dear Mother won't make any fuss."

"When there's more food for the rest of us."

Uly scowled. "That poem's — *hic!* That poem isn't even — *hic!* It — *hic!* It isn't — *hic!*"

He was trying to tell his sisters that the poem wasn't very good — that the birds in the alder trees sang much more interesting songs about battles and hidden caches and daring escapes from predators. But his body betrayed him.

"That poem's — *hic!* — dumb! *Hic!*"

The sisters giggled in delight.

"You'd better not hiccup when Mr. Scratch comes around."

"Better not."

"Otherwise, he'll *find* you."

"He'll catch you in his ashy teeth."

"And that —"

"Will be —"

"The end —"

"Of *Ewwly.*"

The only thing Uly hated more than his nickname was when his sisters talked like this. As if the same dark voice slipped from muzzle to muzzle, using six tongues to speak.

But where that voice came from ... Uly had no idea.

Later that night, their mom dragged dinner into the den and then promptly fell asleep.

The sisters pounced, and the groundhog vanished in a blur of fur and blood. Uly managed to wriggle between their thrashing bodies and snag a bit of something, which he clamped in his muzzle and took back to his corner.

It was nothing but an ear, full of cartilage. But the sisters still stared with jealous eyes and bloody muzzles as he choked it down.

TWO

"Wake up, wake up, my little pups!"

Uly stirred from a hunting dream to find his six sisters bounding toward the den's entrance, which glowed orange and gray. He hefted himself onto his foreleg and hopped after them, but his sisters had formed a half circle, blocking him out.

"You're getting so big, all of you," their mother said outside. "I can barely catch enough food to keep up."

Uly's heart started to sink.

"So tonight," she said, "you're going to hunt your own insects."

The sisters yipped and leapt in excitement, drowning out Uly's whimpers.

He gazed between his sisters' ears and up the stone slope. The Great Boulder shimmered with dawn. It looked so bright and steep that it made his forepaw ache just to

59

look at it. How was he supposed to hunt with only three legs? How was he even supposed to climb up there?

Their mother cleared her throat, and the sisters' yips fell silent.

"You are *not* to venture beyond the crack, do you understand?"

"Yes, Mom," six bored voices said at once.

Uly could see it now. The crack cut high across the Great Boulder like a crooked grin. Every night, the wind blew from the alders to the west and slid along the swell of rock, catching in the crack and howling as if in pain. The crack was just wide enough for a kit to tumble into. And even though he knew it was ridiculous, Uly had a feeling that this was where Mr. Scratch lived.

"Keep within sniffing range," their mother said as Uly's sisters bounded out of the den.

He sat under the arch's shadow, watching as they gekkered across the boulder, ripping at each other's ears and tumbling one another onto the stone. The sight made his whiskers wince.

Uly searched the sky for spiraling shadows. His sisters once told him the story of a mother who walked the Boulder Fields in the bright of evening, her kits trailing behind her. The mother heard a swoop of wings and turned to find that her one and only son was gone — taken into the skies. The hawk had left nothing behind of the kit save his silhouette ... in blood.

A muzzle lay between Uly's ears, making him flinch.

"Everything will come twice as hard for you, Uly, my son," his mom whispered. "But the rewards will be twice as wonderful. Once you finally manage to nip a strawberry, the juice will taste twice as sweet. The prairie dogs will be twice as succulent when you tear open their bellies. And the vixens —" Her voice caught. "Well, life will have a shine for you that it will not have for any other fox. You'll never take anything for granted."

A warmth spread through Uly's chest, stoked by his mother's words.

"Come play with us, Uly!" Agatha called back to the den.

"Yeah!" Ava cried. "Come play so the hawks eat you instead of us!"

Uly flashed a worried look at his mom.

She only smiled. "What hawk would want you? You have no meat on your bones." She nuzzled in his ear and whispered, "I'd be more worried if I were your sisters."

Uly snorted. He licked her on the snout, took a deep breath, and made a small hop out of the den. Its protective shadow slid back, and the sky opened like a giant's eye above him.

He looked back at his mom.

"I'm right here," she said.

With that, Uly romped into the evening with a gait just as confident as his sisters', if a little more lopsided.

The world outside the den felt violent to Uly's senses. His nostrils itched with the dust of tumbling rocks. His eyes burned with sunset, shining bright behind the alders. The boulder still held the day's heat, sizzling the bottom of his forepaw.

He swiveled his ears, searching for insect sounds. But all he could hear was his sisters — wrestling, yipping, and playing tug-of-war with sticks.

62

"First kit to catch a dragonfly is emperor supreme!" Ava screamed.

With that, the sisters bounded into the air, snapping at the swooping blue insects.

Clack!

Clack!

Clack! Clack!

Clack!

Clack!

Uly decided to start simple. He fixed his eyes on the first star of the evening, determined to make his first-ever jump. He made a mighty push off his forepaw, then leapt with his back two paws … and managed to hop about a whisker off the stone. He cowered, waiting to see which sister would start laughing. But they were too focused on the dragonflies to notice him.

Uly focused on the star and tried again. He pushed up off his forepaw, but this time his hind legs leapt too hard, throwing his top half off-balance. He tipped backward, rotating his body only for his muzzle to crack against the hard stone and chomp his tongue.

The laughter came, echoed six times.

Uly rolled onto his stomach, jaw trembling, blood dribbling onto his chin. His mother came to him, as she had dozens of times before. She slid her muzzle under his chest, helping him up onto his forepaw.

"A fox is clever, Uly," she said, "above all, above all. Your sisters may be able to hunt. But in order to survive in the wild, you'll have to think of something that is truly *Uly*."

He glanced toward his sisters, then whispered, "Can't I just stay with you?"

"Oh, honey." His mother gave him a kindly look. "I might not always be here."

His ears flattened as he tried and failed to come up with a way only he could survive. His sisters sprinted and swiveled and skidded, making him think of all the things he couldn't do.

"Come with me," his mom said.

She led him around their den to the low part of the Great Boulder, which smelled of wet soil and fresh green needles. A few tails away, the boulder ended at a jagged drop-off, announcing the start of the forest. The needles of the fir trees brushed the rock's edge, as if they were slowly eating it.

The sisters had told Uly so many terrifying stories about the forest that he couldn't look into its shadows without seeing faces grin back at him.

"Critters are injured every day," his mom said. "Nestlings fall to the ground, babies are abandoned, innards go uneaten. The forest is a feast *if* you know where to look."

Uly sniffed along the boulder's edge, but his nose couldn't seem to catch anything but rock dust. His mom nudged his muzzle toward a light squeaking, which he followed until he caught the warm scent of something tiny and curled. It was a baby squirrel, no bigger than an acorn. It had tumbled out of its drey, high in the pines.

"Congratulations, sweetheart," his mom said. "You're officially a hunter."

Uly opened his mouth to eat the squirrel, but then a breeze made him flinch. He glanced toward his sisters.

"We'll tell them you sniffed it out all by yourself," his mom said. "Can you act like a brave hunter?"

Uly puffed out his chest. *"Like this?"* he said in a scratchy voice.

65

His mother suppressed a giggle. "My little warrior kit."

Uly ate his catch slowly, relishing every bite.

"You're right, Mom," he said, licking his lips. "It did taste twice as good."

"No fair!" Ava called. "Uly's cheating!"

Uly's ears folded as four of his sisters stepped atop the roof of their stone den and stared down at him.

"Mom's hunting for him!" Anna said.

"Actually," his mom said, "Uly found that little morsel himself, didn't you, sweetie?"

"Hic!"

Uly cowered, forgetting to act brave.

"If he can't hunt, he should starve," Ada said.

"It's only fair," said Ali.

"Hush now," their mother said. "How would any of you feel if your sisters talked about you that way?"

Three of the sisters whimpered with guilt.

Only Ava stood strong. "Mr. Scratch wouldn't like what you're doing, Mom."

Uly saw storm clouds pass behind his mother's eyes.

"Ava ... ," she said. "Where on earth did you hear that name?"

Ava stared at her mother, defiant.

"I did it! I did it!" Agatha called.

The sisters turned to see what had happened. Agatha had snagged a dragonfly out of the air. The insect buzzed and coiled, jabbing at her snout with its juicy abdomen.

While their mother and sisters licked her with praises, Uly kept his eyes on Ava. She snuck down to the boulder's edge and stuck her muzzle between the needles ... as if she were looking for someone.

THREE

Skritch

skritch skritch

skritch.

Uly dreamed he was being eaten alive. Tiny creatures nibbled every inch of his skin. He tried to scrape them away with his hind paws, but his forepaw kept slipping and the creatures kept leaping back onto him, sinking in their pine needle-teeth.

Skritch skritch

skritch

skritch skritch
skritch skritch.

Uly scratched himself awake. The creatures were gone, but his skin still felt like it was being eaten. An itch squirmed to life in his ear, and he dug into it, whimpering. Another bloomed on his neck, and he flopped onto his other hip to reach it.

68

"Uly has mites!" Ava whispered.

The six sisters pressed against the den's far wall, eyes wide.

"He's being eaten alive!" whispered Ali.

Uly wanted to argue, but he couldn't stop scratching. He tried balancing upright so he could switch between his hind legs more easily, but his forepaw kept giving out. He rolled onto his back and writhed, scratching at his sides with both hind paws.

"You — *hic!* — made mites — *hic!* — up!" he said.

"Nope," Anna said.

"They're tiny bugs," Ava said.

"They live in your hair."

"*Hundreds* of them."

"They just keep having more and more babies."

"And the babies drink up your blood."

"And eat your skin."

"Soon all your hair falls out."

"And you shrivel up like a rotten peach."

"And eventually, you scratch yourself to pieces and you *die*."

"No! *Hic!*" Uly said, scratching, hiccupping, trying to keep upright. "I — *hic!*—don't — *hic!* — have — *hic!* — m-*hic!* — mites!"

69

"Clearly," Ava said, "you *do*."

Skritch skritch skritch skritch skritch.

Now Uly was trying to scratch away his fear too. Was this Mr. Scratch? Had he finally come for him?

"Ma — hic! — aw — hic! — ooommmm!" he howled.

Their mother stirred in the back of the den. "What is it? Who's crying?"

"Uly has *mites*!" Ava said.

"He stinks so bad he drew them all to us!" said Ada.

"All. Of. Them," Ali said.

"We have to abandon den!" said Anna.

"Hush your muzzles," their mom said. She sniffed at Uly's fur while he continued to scratch. Then she licked the worry from his brow. "There, there, sweetheart. You don't have mites. Your sisters just missed some spots when they cleaned you."

Uly scowled at his sisters, who snickered while his mom gave his fur a thorough cleaning. Her tongue reached deep down to his skin, bringing a flutter to his eyelids. But when she finished, he still felt itchy. He nibbled at his hind legs, convinced he wouldn't feel better until he'd chewed every inch of his fur off.

His mom sighed and trotted to the mouth of their stone den. Uly followed her gaze up the Great Boulder, into the night. His jaw began to tremble. He knew what his mom was going to say, and he wanted to bite her whiskers to keep her from saying it.

"We'll have to take you to the Rain Pool," his mom said. "A quick dip should do the trick."

Uly went so numb he hardly felt the itching anymore. The Rain Pool was beyond the crack.

Ava scoffed. "How's he supposed to swim with only three —"

"Ava," her mother said. "Bite your tongue this instant."

Ava grudgingly shut her muzzle.

"The rest of you are coming with us," their mother said, "and you're going to keep Uly safe, because you didn't do your job as sisters. No fox can clean all the hard-to-reach places by themselves. I'm very disappointed in you."

The sisters hung their heads. Some because they were ashamed. Others to hide their smiles.

Their mom sniffed outside. "It's a good night for a journey. The winds will obscure our scent, and any hawks will be swept off their strike."

She usually avoided taking them out late, when the hawks could spot them under the bright of the moon. Uly was about to tell her he didn't need to go, that he'd learn to live with the scratching. But then a new itch burned to life on his eyelid. And he knew it would drive him to madness, if he didn't scratch himself to pieces first.

"Keep close to my tail now," his mom said.

As Uly pushed up to his paws, Ava pressed her cold snout into his ear. "Watch out for the crack, *Ewwly*."

He snapped at her, but she leapt away, and he barely caught his balance.

"What are you gonna do?" he asked her.

Ava only smiled and joined their sisters at the mouth of the cave. And Uly found himself wishing he could scratch her away like he would an itch.

FOUR

The stars pierced bright and sharp that night. The air was alive with wind.

The kits' mother moved swiftly up the curve of the boulder, and the six sisters followed close. Only Uly trailed behind, stopping every few tails to scratch an itch and search the night sky for winged silhouettes.

They arrived at the crack. The boulder glowed bone white on either side, falling into a darkness that whistled eerie notes into Uly's heart.

Their mother lifted a forepaw and took roll.

"Here!"

"Here!"

"Here!"

"Here!"

"Here!"

73

"Here!"

"Uly?"

"Here," he whispered.

If Mr. Scratch did live in the darkness, Uly didn't want him to know he was there.

Their mother hopped over the crack like it was nothing more than a trickle of water.

"Ava?" she said. "You're alpha. Show your siblings how it's done."

Ava sat down. "I want to make sure Uly gets across safe first, Mom."

Uly's ears folded.

"That's very considerate of you," their mom said. "Ali?"

Ali gave a little scoot backward and then bounded, easily clearing the crack.

Uly glanced at Ava. She smiled.

"Anna?" their mother said.

With a skittering start, Anna made a mighty leap and landed safely on the other side.

Uly was more afraid of Ava than he was of any hawk. The hawks never came into his den and teased him about his sickly paw. They never stole food out of his muzzle.

"Aya."

Aya held her breath, ran, and leapt. Safe.

What was Ava going to do? Wait until Uly tried to jump and then clamp on to his tail so he went tumbling into the crack and she never had to clean him again?

"Ada and Agatha."

The two kits wiggled their hips and then bounded across.

Or did Ava know Mr. Scratch was going to lunge out of the darkness and seize his throat with ashen teeth?

"Okay, Uly," his mom said. "Your turn."

All of the siblings were across the crack except him and Ava. The runt and the alpha.

He stared into the darkness that fell away between him and his mother. His foreleg collapsed, and he fell to his belly.

"Uly," his mother said with a touch of scorn. "You're much too big for me to come and carry you. Come along now."

"Come on, Uly!" Agatha cried. "You can do it!"

"Yeah, jump, jump!"

"Do it before the hawks swoop down and rip out our innards!"

"Stop being such a mewler!"

Uly gave Ava a wary look. She smirked and took a step back. She didn't need to grab his tail for him to slip and fall into the crack. Uly could accomplish that all by himself.

"Eyes on me, Uly," his mother said.

Uly pushed up onto his three paws and scratched at his chest. He gave his mom a determined look, then, before he could second-guess himself, bounded three times. A whisker before the crack, he closed his eyes, pushed off his forepaw, and leapt with his two hind legs. His heart lifted as the darkness passed beneath him. There was a breathless moment of wind.

Uly's forepaw touched down on the other side.

But his hind paws fell away into nothing.

The edge of the boulder struck his stomach, forcing an *oof* from his muzzle. His forepaw started to slip as the weight of his hind legs dragged him backward. Uly whimpered and clawed as he went slipping into the crack ...

Where he plopped onto a vein of mud.

He was in a stone tunnel. Darkness howled around him, broken only by a vein of stars. At the far end of the tunnel was a hole that looked onto the lashing fir trees. Uly heard a faint trickle of water and a low wind that sounded just like breathing —

Teeth clamped onto his scruff and hauled him upward. His mom plopped him, breathless, beside his sisters.

"You did it, Uly!" Agatha called.

"*Psh. Kind* of," Ali said.

The five sisters licked his fur, snickering but happy to see him safe and sound. Trembling, Uly peered back into the crack. From this side, he could see it was no more than a tail deep. He'd never had anything to be afraid of.

"Ha ha ha ha ha!" On the other side of the crack, Ava laughed so hard she could barely breathe. "Uly, you should have *seen* yourself!"

Her laughter rippled to the other sisters.

"Hey, guys!" Ava called to them. "Watch this. Who am I?"

"*Ava ...,*" their mother said, snarling with warning.

Ava curled her left forepaw to her chest. Her right forepaw trembled as she put on a scared face and made a pathetic hop over the crack. Even though she landed safely on the other side, she fell to her belly and pushed herself backward until her hind legs dangled over the ledge, desperately clawing with her right forepaw.

"Ha ha!" laughed Ada.

"Hee hee hee!" said Ali.

"That's exactly what he looked like!" said Aya.

"Come on, Uly!" Anna said, nipping his throat. "You can laugh. It's funny!"

"Ava, watch out!" their mother screamed.

A red-and-yellow king snake struck from the crack, sinking its fangs into Ava's leg. Her yelp echoed across the boulder. Her mother seized her by the scruff and shook until the snake's coiling body came loose. It slithered back into the crack — right where Uly would have stepped if he'd had an extra paw to step with.

Ava's body slumped onto the rock, paws twitching, while their mother whimpered and licked her face. Uly could only watch in shock as the venom spread in veins through Ava's eyes — as her breath grew faster, faster, faster ...

And then slowed. And was gone.

FIVE

The days passed in pinks and golds outside the den.

Now that the sisters were only five, their spell over Uly seemed to have broken. They didn't have Ava's sharp tongue or dark ideas to torment him anymore.

Still, life didn't grow easier for Uly. His skin still itched. His tummy still ached. Ever since Ava had died, the kits' mother had been too grief-stricken to hunt. She spent the days and nights lying with her face toward the stone while Uly's sisters scavenged for themselves. But they managed to catch only beetles and grasshoppers, leaving him nothing but barbed legs and antennae.

Uly wondered: If Ava had survived, would things have been better for him ... or worse?

One night, after his sisters were asleep, Uly crept to the back of the den and curled up beside his mom. He cleaned the tears from her eyes, only stopping to scratch an itch.

He needed her to cheer up. He couldn't hunt by himself. The world felt as big and impossible as it had the day of the dragonfly hunt. His foreleg still trembled when he thought about climbing the boulder or jumping over anything wider than a whisker.

"Mom?"

She didn't stir.

"Mom, I'm hungry."

He listened to her breath, soft and ragged from sobbing. Would she have grieved like this if the snake had bitten him instead of Ava? He scratched another itch.

The light outside was growing hazy. A couple months from now, after the leaves had fallen, his sisters would celebrate their Golden-Eyed Day. They would become vixens and leave the den to sniff out a suitable mate. Shortly before that, boy foxes were meant to have their own Golden-Eyed Day, setting out to mark their own territories.

With only three paws, Uly knew that would never happen for him. But he didn't mind. Once his sisters were gone, he planned to remain in the den with his mom forever.

He cleaned his mom's face, hoping to wake her. He licked her muzzle, her tear-streaked whiskers, her ears ... and he noticed one was missing a tip.

"Mom? How'd you hurt your ear?"

"Your father did that," she whispered without opening her eyes. "It was an accident."

Uly wondered what life would be like if his dad was still alive. Would they have enough food? Would Uly's left foreleg have grown like the others? Would Ava have been nicer to him? Would she still be alive?

"Mom? How did Dad die?"

His mom finally opened her eyes. Something passed behind them. Like storm clouds.

"He fought another fox on a high cliff," she said. "There was a rockslide, and he was buried."

She sighed. "I miss him sometimes. In the twilight. He treated me like a beautiful vixen even though I was old in my years."

Uly giggled. "You're not old" — he quirked his head, noticing the gray tufts of hair in his mom's fur — "are you?"

When she didn't respond, he thought about what *he* would do if he were ever in a fight. Probably hop away at the first snarl.

"Why didn't Dad just run away?" he asked.

"I'll never know." She snorted. "*Dogs.* Promise me you'll never become one."

Uly smiled back. "I promise."

For the first time since Ava had died, his mom gave a small smile. But it faded just as quickly when she saw Uly's ribs poking through his fur.

"You've grown so thin," she said. "I'm sorry."

Uly stared at the ground. "Yeah."

"I'll catch us some food in the morning," she said, laying her head back down.

Uly's stomach gurgled happily. "And I can stay here with you? Forever?"

"Yes, darling," she said. "Forever."

He lay between her paws, and she curled around him, her tail protecting his tail, her muzzle his muzzle, and they fell asleep.

SIX

"Uly!"

Uly woke to the sound of his mom's panicked voice.

"Uly, wake up!" she whispered. "We have to hide you!"

He opened his eyes and found her dragging leaves over his body.

"What? *Why?*"

"Because we're playing a game, my darling!" she said, trying to keep her voice calm. "You're going to play dead, and your sisters are going to try and find you." She pawed leaves over his tail. "Don't move a muscle until I tell you it's safe. Now *hush*, the game is starting."

Uly didn't like the sound of his mom's voice or the look on her face. "Mom, I don't want to play a game. I want *food*."

"Hush now. Do as I say."

Uly whimpered as she pawed leaves over his head. He tried to lie quietly, but his heart wouldn't stop pounding. He watched, wide-eyed, through the cracks in the leaves.

Outside, dawn bloomed rosy and strange. A westerly wind blew along the boulder, and it carried a new scent. Beneath the pine was something like ... *lilac*.

Uly's sisters lined up near the den's entrance. He'd never seen them sit so still.

"Keep quiet about your brother now," his mom whispered to the sisters.

"Why?" asked Aya.

"Yeah," said Ali, "who cares about *Ewwly*?"

"Not me," said Ada.

"Not any —"

A shadow darkened the entrance, and the sisters fell silent.

Uly blinked. It was a fox. At first, all he could make out was a silhouette — two sharp shoulder blades angling toward sharp ears. But then he squinted through the leaves and saw bright amber eyes, a muzzle streaked black, and two white fangs like moons in their waning.

86

His mother bowed. "I thought you were dead."

And Uly knew that this fox was his father.

The fox tilted up his nose. "How pleasantly surprised you must be."

"Yes," his mother said, her jaw trembling. "I am."

The fox examined the den with the lights of his eyes. "Are you going to invite me in?"

"Yes," she said, glancing toward Uly beneath the leaves. "Please. Come in."

The fox padded inside, wafting his lilac scent. Uly thought he'd be excited to see his father alive and in their den. But instead he was conscious of every bit of his own fur that might be showing through the leaves. He wasn't sure why.

The fox walked up and down the line of sisters, sniffing. "This is your litter?"

"Yes, this is all of them," their mother said, breathless. "Five."

"Where is the clever one? Ava, was it?"

"Killed," his mother said. She swallowed deeply. "Bitten by a king snake. How did you know —"

The fox huffed, interrupting her. He sniffed toward the pile of leaves where Uly was hidden. "Where is the cripple?"

Uly's mom was shocked into silence a moment. "He's ... also dead," she said, her breath shallow. "Starved in the night."

"Ah." The fox's whiskers curled into a smile. "Good." He padded the den's perimeter. "Shame about Ava. She was an obedient kit. She followed my instructions for what to do with a crippled runt. You steal its food until it starves."

Uly remembered the song his sisters had sung.

Mr. Scratch is made of ash.

Mr. Scratch has teeth that gnash.

Gobbles all the litters' runts.

Tiny kits are what he hunts.

Dear Mother won't make any fuss

When there's more food for the rest of us.

And Uly realized that his father was Mr. Scratch.

"You ... spoke to Ava?" his mom asked.

Mr. Scratch smiled. "When you left me to die beneath those rocks, my anger kept me alive. Over time, I managed to dig myself out and track your scent across the long miles." His amber eyes fixed Uly's mom to the spot. "And I finally found you."

Uly's mom tried to smile. But her lips were shaking.

Mr. Scratch marched up and down the line of sisters, sniffing at their fur, their ears. "I have been visiting the base of this boulder at night. Watching. Checking to ensure you have remained loyal to me."

He found a bit of mud on Agatha's paw and sneered until she licked it away. He continued to the entrance and looked out across the rock. "Ava saw me in the alders one night. And I have been whispering life's secrets to her ever since. She was to inform me when she and her siblings celebrated their Golden-Eyed Day, so I could collect what is rightfully mine." His eyes flashed to Uly's mom. "And bring you home with me."

Uly bit his tongue to keep from whimpering. His mom couldn't leave. She was supposed to stay there with him forever. She'd promised.

Mr. Scratch smiled at the sisters. He turned to exit the den but then peered back over his shoulder. "Once these kits have grown, you will return to the Lilac Kingdom."

Uly's mom hung her head. "I'll return."

Uly started to tremble, rattling the leaves. When his sisters left the den in autumn, would his mom really leave him to fend for himself? She'd promised he could stay with her forever. She —

"Hic!"

A silence cut through the den.

"Hic!"

Uly folded his forepaw over his muzzle to stop his hiccups, but it only made them worse.

"Hic! Hic! Hic! Hic!"

Mr. Scratch sniffed. "Does it live?" he asked, slow and dangerous.

"No," Uly's mom said. "That was me. I ..."

Mr. Scratch padded to the back of the den and pawed the leaves from Uly. He scowled at Uly's wilted foreleg. Uly couldn't stop hiccupping.

"This," Mr. Scratch said to Uly's mom, "cannot be here."

She started to shake. "Wynn. He's only two moons old. One of his legs didn't grow right. He can't leave. He won't *survive*."

"Who said anything about leaving?" Mr. Scratch said. "I want you to break its neck."

Uly's mom looked horror-struck. "Wynn. *Please.*"

Uly couldn't do anything but tremble and hiccup.

Mr. Scratch sighed. "A vixen who births something this pathetic must be the one to take care of it." He nodded toward Uly. "Do it now."

Uly's sisters started to whimper. Uly cowered in the leaves. His mom didn't move.

"Very well," Mr. Scratch said.

He lunged across the den. There was a flash of white, a sharp snap, and then the tip of Agatha's ear was dangling. Blood trickled down her cheek.

Mr. Scratch cast a shadow over the five sisters. "I will give you a choice," he said to their mother. "You can keep the five girls or that crippled boy. Choose quickly or I'll kill them all."

Uly's mom looked from Uly to his sisters. "No. No, you can't make me —"

Mr. Scratch took Agatha's throat in his mouth and twisted. She whimpered and trembled, blood dripping from her ear.

Uly met his mom's eyes. Tears streamed down her cheeks.

"Mom?" he said.

"I ...," she said. "I choose ..."

Before she could say it, Uly ran from the den. He hopped up the slick rock of the Great Boulder, claws skidding, whimpering every time his forepaw struck the hard stone. Every few steps, he stumbled, bruising his muzzle. But then he'd sense an ashen shadow behind him, and his fear would pick him up again.

Uly reached the crack and hesitated. But then he heard ragged breath on the wind. He leapt. Again, his stomach struck the far edge. Again, his forepaw clawed desperately as his hind legs dragged him down.

He struck the mud and found himself back in the howling tunnel. Red and yellow scales coiled wetly through the rock. Without his mother there to drag him out, Uly couldn't reach the crack of sky above.

At the end of the tunnel, he saw the opening onto the fir trees. He heard the rush of water, the swish of needles.

He ran until the rock came to an abrupt end. Muddy water spilled around his forepaw and over a ledge, trickling down a hundred tails into a shallow pool below. He stared at the drop as the darkness howled behind him. He could sense Mr. Scratch's muzzle snarling through the crack, snipping toward his ears.

Uly didn't so much jump as slip off the ledge. He fell and fell and fell until his body smacked the water, and everything went dark. He flipped and rolled and spun in circles as he scrabbled for the surface. His forepaw caught on something solid, and he dragged himself, dripping, onto shore, where he flopped, gasping, onto his side.

Once his breath came easy again, he pushed himself upright. His eyes climbed the cliff. He expected to find Mr. Scratch perched atop the Great Boulder. But there was no one there.

Uly blinked the mud from his eyelashes. The ragged breath, the ashen shadow — it had all been his imagination. His own fear had chased him into the crack and off the cliff. And now he'd never get back to his den again.

He was about to howl for his mom, but his throat tightened. If Mr. Scratch heard him, he might leap down and end Uly's life.

Uly gazed into the alders — the faces in the shadows. And deciding the trees were less terrifying than his father, he hopped into the forest.

He would wait until the winds cleaned the lilac scent from the boulder and his mom called down that it was safe to come out again. She'd find a way to guide him back up the cliff. Even if she had to leap down and carry him by the scruff.

Uly didn't go far into the forest. Only a few foxtails, where his mom could still catch his scent. He found a mossy spot and plopped, wet and exhausted, onto his stomach.

No one was there to nuzzle him upright again.

"THIS STORY IS DUMB," the fourth kit said, pushing up on his trembling paws. "No dad would ever try and kill his son. And even if he tried, the mom would stop him." His voice was shaking. "This story is unrealistic and — and dumb and — and — and — and — and *dumb*."

With that, he padded back toward the den to snuggle his mom ... just to make sure.

Five little foxes.

The sky above the Antler Wood was the color of rotting pumpkins now. A chill crept into the little one's paws.

"Wait," the fifth kit said. "What happened to Uly?"

"Patience," the storyteller told him, eyes flashing in the shadows of the cavern.

"Why were his sisters so mean to him?" the beta asked.

"They lived in a land where food was scarce," the storyteller said. "Who knows? If the Antler Wood ran dry and the berries vanished, and even the measliest of morsels was swept up by the owls, you might try and starve your siblings too."

The five kits gave one another doubtful looks. Their bellies were full with muskrat and earthworm.

"You promised this story would be scary," the third kit said.

"Shh!" said the beta. "You're going to make it worse!"

"I cannot make it better or worse," the storyteller said. "Only tell you what happened."

The third kit wrinkled her muzzle. "Fine."

The storyteller sighed, and the breeze blew cold. "There are creatures who live in the wood but do not belong there. They're as tall as trees but skinny as sticks. And their hairless skin is as pale as bone."

A figure bloomed in the little one's mind.

"They're cold and lonely, these creatures," the storyteller said. "Some might steal a fox's skin for warmth. Others might do something much, much worse ..."

A branch snapped in the wood. The little one tried not to look.

HOUSE OF TRIX

ONE

"Do I get to be red like you now that I'm grown up?"

Mia followed her mom's tail through the Vole Fields while trying to examine her own dusty-brown paws. She thought her fur might be changing color, but her paws wouldn't hold still long enough for her to tell.

"Red fur will come with time," her mom said.

"Oh." Mia blinked. "What about my eyes? Is the blue gone yet?"

Her mom stopped walking just long enough to give Mia's nose a lick. "Not yet, dear heart. Now come along."

"Okay, okay."

Her mom slipped through the wind-woven vines, and Mia followed, nosing through the tangle until the leaves came to an abrupt end and the world opened like a gasp. The sky beamed upon an emerald meadow. A soft wind blew pale stripes across the grass, sweeping as far as Mia's eyes could see.

"Whoa," she said, then caught an itch behind her ear. "Do I have to have babies?"

"That's not for many months yet," her mom said. She slipped into the meadow's high grasses, leading them down a shadowy passage. "And only then if you want them."

"Where do I get them even?" Mia asked.

Her mom was distracted, sniffing for danger.

"Bizy said babies grow on a blackberry bush in winter," Mia continued. "And you have to pick them *verrry* carefully or else they'll pop and get milk all in your mouth."

"Bizy said that, did she?"

"Yeah. But I could tell she was faking." Mia sneezed when a blade of grass poked her in the nostril. *"Was* she faking?"

"Yes," her mom said. "If you want kits, then ... well, they will come to you."

Mia imagined a small bundle sailing in from the horizon on a fluffy dandelion seed. She imagined the bundle landing before her paws and unfolding into a squirming pink litter.

"Do I ever have to eat grasshoppers again?" she asked.

The questions persisted as Mia and her mom crossed the meadow, keeping hidden in the thicker patches. Every so often, her mother stopped and lifted a paw, sniffing back the way they'd come. Mia lifted a paw and sniffed too.

"What are we looking for?" she whispered.

"Hush," her mom said, ears alert.

Mia waited patiently until her mom set down her paw and continued on.

It felt strange, traveling away from the Eavey Wood — away from the kindly sights and scents, the soil and leaves that crunched familiar underpaw. It was strange knowing that she would not be returning to the den that night to curl up in a fuzzy pile with her brothers and sister.

The thought pinched something in Mia, and she gazed back through the grasses — past the hills and the valleys toward home.

"Eyes ahead, Mia, my love," her mom said. "Foxes don't look back to their kithood den once they're grown. They have to show the other kits — the ones who didn't pass the test — what it means to be brave." Her mom's voice caught, like it had hooked on a thorn.

"Okay, Mama," Mia said.

She nibbled an itch from her tail, where Miss Vix's teeth had plucked the hairs, and then bounded after her mom's sweet apple scent.

TWO

As dusk dusted the horizon, Mia and her mother arrived at the mouth of a forest. The trees bristled and smelled of sap. Their needles clawed the sky.

Her mom bounded into the wood, dissolving in shadow, but Mia's bottom plopped onto a mossy hump. Her paws refused to budge.

Fox eyes weren't meant for forests. Every kit knew that.

We keep to the edges of things, Miss Vix had told Mia and her siblings. *Between field and forest. Between meadow and wood. There you'll find places for hiding, the rodents and insects are as plentiful as stars, and the sky is thrown so wide you'll smell a hawk or a hunter approaching from miles away.*

"Mia?" her mom's voice said from the shadows.

Mia whimpered, then bit her tongue, remembering she was grown-up now.

Her mom bounded out of the trees and tried to nuzzle Mia's chin, but Mia couldn't stop staring into the forest.

"*Darling*," her mom said in a calm voice, "once we make it to the other side of these trees, we can hunt and rest."

Even though she wasn't supposed to, Mia looked back the way they'd come. She'd feel a lot better if she could just tease Roa one last time. Tackle Marley. Chew on Alfie's ears.

"Why can't we just go back to the Eavey Wood?" she asked.

"*Because*," her mom snapped, "I said so."

Mia's ears flattened, and her mom's eyes filled with guilt. "I'm sorry, Mia. This isn't your fault." She sniffed at the trees. "This forest is shallow." *Snff snff.* "I can smell a peach grove on the other side." *Snfffff.* "Ooh, and it has a centipede infestation!"

Mia's belly gurgled. Centipedes were her favorite food, especially when found in an overripe peach.

"Come now," her mom said, bounding back into the trees. "You're too big for carrying."

"But, but, but …" Mia's paws kneaded the dirt.

What if the yellow stench was in there? Her mom had told her it was all a test, but she couldn't quite make herself believe it. What if the yellow was watching from the shadows with its gooey eyes and dripping saliva, waiting to bite her tail again?

There came a sigh, and then her mom trotted back into the light of dusk. "Okay, Mia. You win. We'll go around. The long way."

"Really?" Mia's bottom came unstuck from the ground, and she followed her mom east along the edge of the forest. "For real?"

"Yes, yes. You've talked me into it. I've lost enough kits today."

Mia's heart squeezed. "What do you mean 'lost'? We know where they are. They're with Miss Vix. In the Eavey Wood."

"Of course," her mom said, not meeting Mia's eyes. "I'll go back for them once — well, once we find our new den." She trotted a little faster.

"Will I get to see them again?" Mia asked, leaping to catch up.

Her mom didn't answer any more questions for a while.

As the sky went softly to sleep, Mia and her mom traced the shadows that wobbled along the edge of the pines. Soon, they came to an odd sight that stopped her mom in her tracks.

The thing looked like a river, but it had no water or stones, and it wasn't running. It lay flat and black along the forest's edge, as straight as a frightened tail.

"What's that?" Mia asked, sniffing.

"A road," her mom said, eyes wide with fear. "We must leave this place. Now."

Mia looked back into the forest, the only other place to go. "But *Mama* —"

"End of argument."

Mia clamped her muzzle shut, catching a whimper. Her mom crept into the trees, and Mia followed as night fell and the shadows closed around them.

■■■■

The path through the forest was twisted and bumpy and barely lit by starlight. Mia tripped over sticks and stepped into holes and was poked in the eyes by leaves. She had to squint to see her mom's tail. She desperately wanted to latch her muzzle on to it, but she fought the urge. She wasn't a kit anymore.

Just when Mia thought the trees would never end, they arrived in a clearing. Mia blinked. Branches swayed against a starry sky. The ground was littered with silver roots.

"Did we make it?" she asked, her heart hopping with relief. "Is this the other side?"

"No, honey," her mom said, sniffing. "I'm afraid we still have a ways to go." She bounded over one silver root and slid under another. She sniffed the air, took another step, and — *crack!* She leapt into the air with a scream. A silver root had bitten her paw.

"Snake!" Mia shouted. She bounded and snapped the thing up in her mouth.

109

But its skin was as solid as stone and woke the nerves in her teeth. Her mom jumped and jerked and spun, trying to escape. Mia shook the silver thing's body with her muzzle. But its jaws clung tight.

Her mom slumped onto her side, paw still trapped.

"Mia," she said, her voice shaking. "Mia, it isn't a snake."

The silver thing hung cold and heavy in Mia's mouth. She let it drop with a clink. She sniffed at the circles of its body, its toothless jaws, her mom's paw all smashed up inside.

"Mama, what is it?"

Her mom shifted her paw, sucking through her teeth. "I don't know."

Mia scratched at it. "Is it ... *dead*?"

"I don't think it was ever alive."

"Then ..." Mia swallowed. "Then how we gonna kill it?"

Her mom didn't answer. She nibbled at her trapped paw, trying to pull it free. But the silver jaws held fast, and she let out a whimper.

Mia's ears lay flat. She'd never heard her mom make that sound before.

110

"Here, Mia," her mom said. "Stick your nose in the narrow part of its mouth. Maybe we can force it open by —"

A branch snapped in the darkness. A light flashed across the leaves. Mia and her mom crouched low as a creature, bigger than anything Mia had seen before, stepped between the trees.

"Watt treeks awake bee Trigses, hmm?"

The voice was high and twisted, and squirmed into Mia's ears.

Mia's mom limped beneath a nearby bush, dragging the silver root with her. Mia slipped in after her, then sniffed toward the creature. It smelled of ... *nothing.*

"Mama?" she whispered. "What is it?"

"Quiet," her mom said, breathless.

Heavy steps crunched through the underbrush. The creature stopped twenty tails away. Its light slid across the leaves until it landed on the bush that held her and her mom.

"Ah!" the voice screeched. *"Icko fogses! Butter 'n awesomes. Ice 'n rose."*

The light shined so bright Mia feared she'd never see darkness again.

THREE

The air pulsed with Mia's heartbeat as the creature clomped toward her and her mom. It was as tall as a sapling and seemed to be having trouble getting through the dense forest.

"Fickle stigs!" it screeched. *"Knacksy branshes!"*

"Mama," Mia whispered.

"Quiet."

"Can it fit in here?"

"Hush, Mia!"

She led her to another nearby bush, dragging the silver root, just before the creature broke through the branches and swept its light around the clearing.

"Weird jewel glow," it whined. *"Coal mouth, coal mou-outh!"*

"Mia, you must run," her mom whispered. "Go. Now. Hide among the trees."

"Mom, no, I —"

"Once everything's quiet, you must continue to the far side of the forest and find a den. Sniff for sandy loam, a sipping creek, and an entrance with good cover. Just like we had in the Eavey Wood. Do you understand?"

Mia's paws were too numb to move. It was her fault they'd come this way. She'd refused to enter the trees when her mom first asked, forcing them to travel where the silver roots bit down and never let go.

"Through the forest? Alone? I ... I can't. Mama, you have to come with me."

Her mom shifted a paw, making the silver root clink. "I can't come with you, Mia."

"But — but you said you'd be there. Every step of the way. You — you lied to me."

"I'm sorry, Mia. I never meant to lie." Her mom's golden eyes searched Mia's blue swirl ones in the flashes of approaching light. "But you have to go. You're the only kit left."

"What do you mean 'the only'?" Mia asked.

The creature tromped closer, burbling. It was ten tails away now.

"Mia," her mother said in a calmer voice now. "Listen to me carefully. Sometimes there are fires in the fields. Many animals will inhale the smoke. Many will die."

The words made Mia tremble. "Why are you telling me this?"

"Hush and listen. From the ashes, the wood and the grasses will grow back lusher, greener than before. They'll be populated with more things to eat. So while some animals may have died, later generations will live better for it. Do you understand?"

Mia couldn't keep her jaw from shaking. "Mama ..."

Her mom licked her cheek. "Tell me you understand."

The thing crunched closer. *"Whiffs at a smell toy sigh ear?"*

"I ... I understand," Mia said.

"Good." Tears streamed down her mom's cheeks. "Now run! Run as fast as your paws can carry you!"

Mia bounded out of the bush. But then she felt a tug on her heartstrings. She

114

nuzzled under a large leaf and peeked out from under it. If she left, then the creature who smelled of nothing would get her mom. Mia couldn't let that happen. She couldn't leave someone in her family behind again.

The thing stomped into the clearing. *"Warty knot! Trigs's ear!"*

By the glow of the floating light, Mia finally saw the thing. It had no fur on its face or paws. Loose skins flapped around its body, and — her heart jerked — the thing walked on two legs. Mia knew what it was now. *Human.*

It's no use being a clever paws around a human, Miss Vix had said. *They are cleverer by a landslide. They will catch you with their traps, peel off your skin with their long fingers, and wear it around their naked necks to keep warm. If you ever see a human, run.*

The human shined its light, following the silver root straight to the bush that hid Mia's mom. A growl awoke in Mia's throat as the human's hairless paws parted the leaves, unveiling her mom's red fur. Her mother snarled and yipped, jerking back, trying to get as far away from the human as she could.

"Water dull lite," the human said, rubbing its paws together.

No, not paws. *Hands.* With five fingers each, every one as deft as a baby snake. The human pulled out two hand skins and slid them over its own. It reached into the bush, and Mia's mom lashed, sinking her fangs into the skin covering the human's hand.

The human didn't so much as wince, only clucked its tongue. *"Imp fat 'n pennies!"*

The growl grew in Mia's throat as the human forced her mom's muzzle to the ground with one hand, using the other to draw a gleaming splinter from the silver root's mouth. Her mom's paw came free, and the human hefted her into the air by the scruff.

Mia's growl grew into a howl. "Let go of my mom!"

She shot out from under the leaf and attacked the human's foot. The human made a surprised *"Woop!"* and dropped Mia's mother to the ground. Mia didn't stop attacking. The foot's skin was as tough as bark. But if she could just bite hard enough, rip hard enough, she was confident she could kill it.

116

"Mia!" her mom shouted. "Let go! Run!"

Mia tried to let go of the human's foot, but her fangs caught on something stringy. Before she could untangle them, fingers seized her by the scruff, making her whole body freeze. And then she was being hefted into the air — up, up, up, high as the branches.

Mia dangled in front of the human's hideous face. It was made of loose frog-belly skin that wiggled and stretched in strange, terrifying ways.

"Wei, wei ... icko morso." The human breathed its strange sounds at her. *"Otter'z breezed! Hee hee."*

With her scruff pinched, Mia could only snarl.

Below, her mom ripped at the loose skin around the human's legs. The human kicked her in the teeth, but her mom shook off the blow and bit down again.

Mia's stomach lifted as the human swooped down to catch her mom with its other hand. But her mom dodged into the brush.

"Verilell!" the human said, standing.

It tried to step away, but Mia's mom kept nipping at its feet. Whenever the human

117

reached down to grab her, she bounded off into the brush.

Finally, the human crouched low, holding Mia out. *"Flair, eh?"* it said. *"Allures."*

With its other hand, it reached toward Mia's mom. Mia's mom remained frozen behind the leaves, her injured paw curled to her chest.

"Mama!" Mia cried. "Don't let it take me!"

Her mom whimpered. She kept her distance.

The human sighed. *"Verilell."*

It hefted Mia as high as the branches again and burbled as it carried her through the forest. Her mom limped behind them, trying to keep up on her injured paw.

"I'll find you, Mia!" her mom called. "Be brave!"

But Mia was too numb with fear to be anything.

Soon her mom's sobs and sweet apple scent were swallowed by the leaves.

FOUR

An orange light bloomed through the elder trees. It shone from something that looked like a den but was built aboveground. Its walls were made of stones and fallen trunks. It had a roof of dead grass. Black smoke billowed from its top, hazing the air and stinging Mia's eyes.

"Housatrix!" the human cried.

Something was wrong with this place. No crickets chirped. No frogs croaked. There were no scuffles in the underbrush. As if the creatures of the wood knew to keep quiet here.

The human carried Mia into the den and then closed it with a click, cutting off the scent of the trees. The walls danced with flames — a forest fire, somehow contained within a small cave. Mia had only ever seen fire from a distance when lightning struck the Great Crook Tree.

119

This close, the crackling flames burned her nose and dried her eyes, making the shapes of the den blur together. She started panting with fear.

"Fur sings fur," the human said.

Mia felt a snip behind her ear as the human stole a tuft of her hair. Then, carrying her by the scruff, it brought her to a nest of silver sticks. The sticks opened with a squeak and Mia fell inside. Another squeak, and she found herself trapped. She tried to bite through the sticks, but they were made of the same impossible stuff as the root that had bitten her mom's paw.

The human unfolded the outer skins from its body, releasing a scent like melting flowers. Its long white fingers hung the skins, one by one, on a dead brown tree. It turned, firelight flickering on its flat, naked face. Raspberries stained its lips. Blueberries tinted its eyelids. A clump of silver hair sat atop its head, and it wore a golden flower at its throat.

Mia sniffed. This human was female.

"Ahh," the woman said in a breathy, bright voice. "Much better."

Mia's ear twitched. She could understand the human now. But how?

The woman drew close and bared her teeth through the silver sticks. "Hello there." She tapped the air a whisker from Mia's muzzle. "I'd reach into your cage and pet you, but I'm afraid you'd nip my finger, you're shaking so."

Mia howled for her mom. *"Aroooroooroooroooroooooooo!"*

"Oh, bup bup bup," the woman said. "None of that now." Her round pupils moved up and down, taking in Mia's coat. "You're a ... *vixen*, I believe." She wrinkled her nose. "Though I won't do either of us the indignity of checking."

She walked to what looked like a hollow tree trunk and drew out something sharp and hooked — a silver claw that gleamed like moonlight on water.

"You were a surprise, you know," the woman said. "And not a pleasant one, I'm afraid."

She picked up a stone and ran it along the claw's edge — *shink shink shink.* The sound raised Mia's hackles.

"I'm not particularly partial to foxes," the woman continued. "They're *unpleasant* creatures at the best of times. Always murdering innocent ducks and mouses and little cherubs — that's what I call piglets, by the way." *Shink shink shink.* "That's why foxes have always been the villains in my stories. Don't much appreciate villains myself."

Mia kept her eyes on the silver claw. She was trying to follow the woman's words, but they didn't make any sense. Stories? Villains?

"Besides," the woman said, "I already have a fox story. *The Tale of Mr. Tod.* And it was not popular amongst the littles." She set down the stone and gave the sharp end of the claw a prick with her nail. "I was hoping to catch a chubby chipmunk or a bunny or perhaps some pleasant forest critter I haven't written about yet."

She brought the claw to the cage. Mia cowered. There was nowhere to hide.

"My, but you *are* beautiful, aren't you?" the woman said, hesitating. "And *young*. Why, you're nothing but a kit!" She tapped the claw against the silver sticks of Mia's cage, thinking. "Perhaps it is time for another fox story. My publisher might enjoy one that isn't so ... well, *nasty*." She set down the claw with a clatter. "Let's give it a try, shall we?"

Mia's ear twitched. Give what a try? Was the woman not going to steal her skin?

"How impolite of me!" the woman said, clapping her hands together. "I haven't made introductions!" Her face drew too close to the cage again. "My name is Beatrix Potter."

Mia's ears flattened. She didn't care about the woman's name. She just wanted to leave.

The woman tapped her lips, studying Mia's face. "And I believe I'll call you ... *Little Miss*."

Mia avoided the woman's eyes as Miss Potter again bared her teeth.

"I am going to make it so that you live *forever*."

FIVE

After Miss Potter sang a bright "Good night" …

After she banished the lights with a click …

After the fire died with a crackle …

It was only then that Mia was able to take in her surroundings. She pressed her nose between the silver sticks of her cage, trying to sniff out an escape. Moonlight poured through a hole in the den's wall. But she couldn't smell the trees or her mom's apple-scented fur. The wind and all its smells were held back by something as invisible as a fly's wing.

Mia searched the den's other walls and found that they were impaled with forest things: mushrooms and feathers and leaves of different shapes; a hairy vine coiled in a circle. There were creatures too: a yellow beetle no longer marching, a butterfly that

did not flutter, as well as a bat, a frog, and a lizard, all shriveled and still. The creatures were as scentless as dust, and Mia's stomach did not rumble at the sniff of them.

She turned her nose upward to see if the den had a top exit, and her heart turned over. There, standing on a flat perch high in the den was a large male fox.

Keep away from unknown foxes, Miss Vix had warned. *If you don't belong to them, they will snap your neck and leave your body for the worms.*

Mia didn't want her neck snapped. But the fox wouldn't be able to reach her in the cage. Besides, who else was going to help her?

"Excuse me?" Mia whispered to the fox.

He didn't respond — only stood proudly, sandy whiskers alert.

"Hello?" she said.

The fox gazed out over the den, eyes gleaming like black currants. He didn't so much as blink.

"Sorry to interrupt." Mia gulped. "You look very, um, *busy,* but I just need to find a way out of this nest. My mom's looking for me outside."

A long silence followed.

"No use talking to him."

"Who's there?" Mia asked, searching the moonlit room. "Who said that?"

"Just me," a pinched voice said.

Mia sniffed but couldn't smell anything. She swiveled her ears until she caught the creature's whistling breath, its slow-thumping heartbeat. Her eyes adjusted to the darkness in the corner, and she saw another silver cage like hers. Faint moon-light made squares on floppy ears, wide eyes, and brownish-gray fur.

"Why can't I smell you?" Mia asked the rabbit.

"That's what she does to you," he said in a tired voice. "She keeps us in these cages, feeding us nothing but oatmeal until our fur loses the smell of the forest."

"Oh." Mia's heart pounded, flooding her head with more questions. "Why can't I smell the trees? How can I understand the human? Why can't I break these sticks?"

The rabbit pointed his nose toward the hole in the den. "That's a window. It cannot be opened. Not by us anyway. Only way out is through that door, there."

127

Mia sniffed at the entrance where Miss Potter had carried her in. It was blocked by a piece of wood that had shut with a click.

"She rarely opens it," the rabbit said. "And she closes it twice as quickly." He sniffed. "As for why we can understand her, I don't rightly know. It was all gobbledygook and gibberish to my ears until she stole a bit of my fur." He sniffed. "That was before she killed Sara."

Mia gulped. "Who's ... Sara?"

"My wife," the rabbit said.

Something stirred inside Mia, but it was faint. It was difficult for her to feel pity for a rabbit. They died all the time. It was part of their nature.

She decided to ask the question she feared the most. "Why won't the fox talk to me?"

The rabbit's eyes shined. "Mr. Tod is not in his body anymore."

She looked at the fox, sitting perfectly still on the high perch. "Wh-what do you mean?"

"He's there," the rabbit said, pointing his nose. "In the *pages*."

On the wall above Mia's cage were several white leaves. The pages, as the rabbit had called them, had markings that showed a bit of nature — trees and rivers and skies — all captured in watery hues.

The pages held a depth Mia felt she could leap into. She could escape the human den and go bounding down the little stone pathways, through a tunnel of brambles, past a field of carrots ... And yet, the pages were as flat as leaves.

"What do you mean the fox is there?" Mia said, staring at the strange little worlds. "Where?"

"In the page farthest from you."

Mia squinted at the wall facing her. These pages were populated with creatures — a bullfrog, a bunny, a squirrel — as flat as the worlds that held them. But they weren't behaving like animals. They stood upright on their hind paws and wore extra skins just like the human.

A duck wore a blue circle around her shoulders and carried a small nest of apples. A frog wore all white and used a long stick to whip a fish out of a pond. A badger wore gray and red skins and walked with a stick in his forepaw. He had a soft expression, which Mia knew was impossible for a badger.

Mia saw the fox with the sandy whiskers — trapped in a page. He wore a green skin around his chest and forelegs, and rested a forepaw on the shoulder of a dim-witted-looking duck.

"Miss Potter doesn't like animals the way they are," the rabbit said. "So she changes them. Makes them more like her." He pointed his nose toward a pile of sharpened sticks. "She starts by stealing your essence with her pencils. Once she's used them to draw you into her story, she'll have no more use for your body." He nodded toward the tree trunk at something floppy and white. "She'll use that cloth to steal your breath. Then she'll pull off your skin and stuff it full of grass. And finally she'll remove your eyes and replace them with shiny rocks."

The fox's gaze glowed darkly above Mia's cage. She looked away.

"After that," the rabbit said, "you'll be trapped in Miss Potter's stories forever. That's what happened to Sara. She's the Nice Gentle Rabbit now."

Mia stared at the fox on the page. He wasn't moving. Wasn't breathing. His whiskers didn't twitch. He just stood, frozen, wrapped in skins, unable to take his paw from the head of the dim-witted duck. Unable to hunt her.

It was the same for the toad, who would never catch the fish. The duck, who would never eat the apples. And Sara, the Nice Gentle Rabbit, poking her nose out of the greenery — unable to do anything but wait for her husband to join her.

If Mia went to the watercolor world, then she'd never see her mom or siblings again.

She shook the thought from her head. Rabbits were scared of everything. Their hearts were always in a panic, their eyes always wide with shock.

"Tell me the truth, rabbit," she snarled, trying to sound more frightening than frightened. "Or else I-I'll rip out your throat."

The rabbit gave her a pitying look, and Mia realized there wasn't a bit of fear in his droopy eyes. "I was like you once," he said. "I kicked and kicked at my cage until I thought my legs might break. Then Miss Potter filled my belly with oatmeal, and it made me old and slow."

Mia looked at the fox with the sandy whiskers. "Tell me he's lying!"

The fox's eyes only glowed.

"Once Miss Potter finishes drawing your story," the rabbit said, "that's when you'll know it's your time."

"No!" Mia attacked the sticks with renewed energy. "I have to get out of here! My mom's out there!"

The rabbit tucked his paws under his chest, warming them from the night. He turned his nose toward the pages lying on top of his cage. "She finished my story this afternoon. Tomorrow, she'll bring the jar and the cloth, and then I'll become just like Mr. Tod." He lay in his cage, turning his back to Mia. "At least I'll be with Sara again."

Mia's breath grew short. Was that how she would end up? Stuck inside one of these watercolor worlds forever? Her skin stuffed, her glowing eyes staring out the window, waiting for her mom to come and find her?

"Wait," Mia called to the rabbit. "How do I get out of here?"

But the rabbit was fast asleep.

SIX

A sound drew Mia out of sleep.

Dawn shined through the speckles of the window, glinting off the silver sticks of her cage. She remembered where she was.

An angry grunt made her sit upright. Miss Potter was crouched over the rabbit's cage.

"There, there, now," the woman said, slipping on her hand skins. "No use in fussing."

Mia's heart started to thrum in her throat.

Miss Potter reached into the rabbit's cage and hefted him out by his floppy ears. His legs kicked. His heart thumped. His breath ruffled. Normally, the sounds would fill Mia with hunger, but right then it made every one of her hairs stand on end.

"It's okay," Miss Potter cooed to the struggling rabbit. "It will all be okay soon."

She took the brown jar from the tree trunk, along with a loose white something.

The cloth, Mia realized.

With one hand, Miss Potter opened the jar and tipped it onto the cloth. A scent wafted through the den. It tickled Mia's nostrils, making her head feel woozy, her eyelids heavy.

"Here we are," Miss Potter said.

She pressed the damp cloth over the rabbit's nose while turning her head away. The rabbit made a muffled grunting. His legs kicked. His heart thumped faster and faster as his gaze frantically searched the room. He found Mia. She watched in horror as the rabbit's eyelids slowly drifted shut and his legs fell limp. When Miss Potter removed the cloth, his breath was gone, along with his heartbeat.

"Oh," the woman said with a bit of heartbreak. "I do hate it when they make those little sounds." She laid out the rabbit's body and picked up the silver claw.

Mia looked away just as his stomach opened wetly. The room thickened with a

134

steamy red scent, making her teeth clack. But whether out of fear or hunger she wasn't sure.

She looked up through her cage at the fox with the sandy whiskers. The rabbit had been right. Mr. Tod had nothing inside his soul. Miss Potter had trapped him inside a page and then stolen his eyes and stuffed his body with grass.

Mia's heart beat in her ears now. She looked back just as Miss Potter lifted the dripping insides of the rabbit, streams of blood running down her arms.

"Pee-*yoo*," the woman said.

She opened the window with her elbow and then slopped the bunny's innards outside. Mia pressed her nose through her cage, sniffing at the trees, the wind, the soil. This was it. She needed to escape. Otherwise, she'd end up just like Mr. Tod and the rabbit. She could almost feel the cold of the silver claw opening her belly. She gnawed at the silver sticks of the cage, trying to get them to snap. But it was no use.

The bunny's innards disposed of, Miss Potter summoned a small waterfall and cleaned the blood from her hands. Then she stepped to what looked like a black boulder and picked up a small stick. There came a brisk scratch, and a flame gasped to life, tingling Mia's nostrils.

Fire. The human could *make* fire.

Miss Potter grew distracted, using the waterfall to fill a pot big enough for Mia to fit inside. Mia watched as the flame crept down the stick to Miss Potter's fingers. The woman hissed like a snake, jerking her hand, and the flame leapt onto the floor.

"Ack! Ack! Ack!" Miss Potter cried, stamping on the fire until it was extinguished. She went to the window and waved the smoke out with her hands. When that didn't clear it, she opened the front door, wafting fresh air into the den.

Miss Potter wiped the sweat from her forehead. "Oh, *Beatrix*," she said, laughing. "You really can be such a *goose* sometimes! You're meant to cook the *rabbit*, not *yourself*!"

The smoke cleared, and she shut the door and the window. Now all that was left was the trapped air, laced with ash. Mia's nose ached to sniff the trees again.

Miss Potter scratched another flame to life and touched it to the boulder, which

136

whooshed with a circle of fire. She lifted the water-filled pot over it, and soon, steam coiled. Once the water started to bubble, Miss Potter dropped the rabbit's empty skin inside. She created another fire and tossed his glistening meat over it.

The room filled with eye-watering smells. A hunger growled up inside Mia, try as she might to fight it. The rabbit's meat would fill her with energy. She might even be strong enough to break these silver sticks. She paced her cage, whimpering and licking her lips.

"Enough fidgeting, Little Miss!" Miss Potter said. "Your breakfast is coming."

Once the meat had grown crisp and glistening, the woman served it to herself. Then she walked to Mia's cage and opened it with a creak. "Here's your oatmeal."

She set a shell of pale burbling mud next to Mia and then closed the door. Mia sniffed at the oatmeal, then sneezed. It was as scentless as mud. Just like she would become if she ate it.

As Miss Potter feasted on the rabbit's meat, making satisfied sounds and slurping the fat from her fingers, Mia tucked herself into a ball in the corner of her cage.

She had disobeyed her mom and not gone into the forest when she was supposed to. And now she would pay the price. Miss Potter would steal her scent. Then her essence. Then her breath and her skin. The woman would feast on Mia's meat while Mia watched, helpless, from a leaf-flat watercolor world.

The rabbit eaten, Miss Potter cleaned the grease from her hands in the small waterfall and then impaled a new page above the rabbit's empty cage.

"There!" she exclaimed. *The Story of a Fierce Bad Rabbit*! It's far from my best work, but it will pay the bills."

She used a stick to fish out the rabbit's skin from the steaming pot, and then opened the front door and hung it to dry.

Mia stared at the new drawing above the empty cage. The rabbit with the floppy ears fled through the flat world in terror, forever running from some unseen danger. Whatever it was had stolen his tail and whiskers.

Mia could have sworn she saw the drawing's nose twitch.

SEVEN

Night fell, and a spindly moon rose in the window.

Mia pretended to sleep while Miss Potter blew out the tiny flames around the room. Footsteps approached the cage, and the latch squeaked open. Miss Potter clicked her tongue. "What a waste." She removed the uneaten oatmeal and then closed the latch again.

She hadn't noticed that one of Mia's eyes was not perfectly shut.

Once Miss Potter was safely tucked away in her room, Mia sat up. A sliver of moonlight gleamed on the cage's silver latch. She'd watched through the crack in her eyelid as Miss Potter had opened it. All Mia had to do was lift.

She poked her nose through the square directly below the latch and tried to nuzzle it upward. But the space was too tight. The silver sticks cut her muzzle. She pulled her nose out to lick the ache away and realized something. She slid her nose back into the square and licked.

Her tongue lifted the latch.

The cage creaked open, and Mia hunched, waiting to see if the sound had woken Miss Potter. Snoring drifted from the other room. Mia bounded out of the cage and crept across the floor, nails clicking as she sniffed for an escape.

Mr. Tod's glowing eyes seemed to follow her around the room.

"Stop staring at me," she whispered to him.

She padded to the den's entrance. Its latch was much too high to lick open, so she sniffed the narrow space around its edges. She could smell squirrels and acorns and leaves and streams. The breath of the forest was a whisker away, but she couldn't figure out how to reach it.

She caught an apple scent, and her tail started to wag.

"Yaowr!" Mia said, making the smallest yelp she could.

A few moments later, a sniffing came from under the door. *"Mia?"*

"Mom!"

She could smell her mom's breath through the crack beneath the door; the same air pulled between their nostrils.

"Oh, thank goodness!" her mom said, sobbing with relief. "You're alive! I'm sorry it took me so long to find you. I move slowly on three paws. Are you okay?"

"She's gonna take my skin!" Mia said. "She's gonna cook me and replace my eyes and — and — and trap me in one of those ... *pages!*"

"Slow down, honey. You can tell me all about it later. Right now, we need to get you out of there."

Mia scratched at the door, whimpering. "This is the only way out. The rabbit told me before Miss Potter — before she took his ..."

"It's going to be okay, Mia," her mom said, but Mia could hear panic in her voice. "Can you reach that hole? I can't jump with my injured paw."

Mia looked at the window. Maybe the rabbit hadn't been right about everything.

The window was as invisible as a fly's wing. Wings could be crunched. She trotted to the space where Miss Potter had skinned the rabbit. She fixed her eyes on the moon in the window and, bounding across the room, made a great leap.

THUMP!

Her nose struck the wall just beneath the window, surprising a yelp out of her. She recovered and crouched in the shadows of the skin tree, muzzle aching, ears alert. Miss Potter snored in her room.

Mia decided to try again, this time pushing the air out of her lungs so she wouldn't make a sound. She ran and leapt and —THUMP!

She pawed at her bruised muzzle and then returned to the door.

"My legs aren't long enough."

Her mom took a breath. "Can you find another way out?"

Mia sniffed. The only other place was down the hall, in the dark space where Miss Potter went to sleep.

"I can try," Mia said, breath shaking.

"I'll be right here," her mom said.

The door to Miss Potter's room was open just a crack. Mia nuzzled it wider and sniffed the darkness. The woman snoozed softly. There was no window. Mia was about to go back, but then shapes started to form in the shadows. Claws. Fangs. Glowing eyes. The room was filled with dead animals — frozen in hideous poses, eyes popping out of their empty skins.

Mia recognized the characters from Miss Potter's pages. There were the squirrel, the duck, and the bullfrog. There was the badger, claws in the air, jaws locked in an eternal hiss. And there was Sara, the rabbit's wife, eyes sparkling with never-ending fear.

Trembling, Mia backed up. Her tail bumped into something, knocking an object to the ground, where it shattered.

"Hmph?"

The sound stirred Miss Potter, who sat bolt upright. She snatched something from her bedside and clicked it, and a beam of light blared across the room, nearly catching Mia's tail as she slipped out of the door. Mia leapt into her cage and caught the door with her teeth. She yanked back, and the latch clicked shut just as the woman stomped into the room.

The light shined on Mia, making her squint.

"Mia!" Mia's mom called from outside. "Mia, tell me you're okay!"

Miss Potter pointed her light out the window. "Who's making that racket?"

Mia's mom fell silent.

Miss Potter killed the light with a click, scratched her chin, and returned to her room.

Mia trembled in her cage, the image of the empty-eyed creatures still wild in her mind. And not only because they were stuffed. The duck had wings for flying. The badger had jaws for chomping. Even Sara had long legs for kicking. And yet none of them were able to escape before Miss Potter stole their essence and their skins.

What chance did a fox kit have?

144

EIGHT

The sun rose and set in the window more times than Mia could count. The days blended together in a stale blur, slowly leaching the terror from her heart and replacing it with something she'd never felt before: boredom.

Every morning, Miss Potter swept into the room, wafting her melted-flower scent and talking to herself. "Make the tea, make the tea." After the water howled in pain, she would throw open the window to let the weather in. Mia would smell her mom outside, patiently waiting for the night to come.

As sunlight filled the human den, Miss Potter would use the silver claw to sharpen her pencils and then sit before Mia's cage, skritching shapes onto her pages.

Skritch skritch skritch. "I've always said that one must see, smell, and *touch* one's subject." *Skritch skritch.* "*Ahem.* Well, perhaps not *smell* — not when one's subject is a skunk or a badger or some *scandalous* character like that." *Skriiiiiiiitch!* "Still, I've always said to myself, I've said, 'Beatrix, you must know how fog *smells*, how frost *tastes*, before you draw it.'"

Day after day, as Mia watched her own form take shape on the page, she thought she could feel her personality slowly seeping out of her paws.

In the afternoons, Miss Potter placed what looked like clear puddles over her eyes and studied her work. "These are turning out *quite* well, if I do say so myself! And ahead of deadline too! I should be finished with you in just a few more days …"

Mia tried not to think about what this meant. Instead, she lay on her side and watched the branches scratch at the window, trying to remember what it felt like to curl up beneath them.

As the sky began to fade, Miss Potter would serve herself duck or rabbit, and Mia a steaming bowl of oatmeal. The smell of sizzling meat squeezed Mia's stomach until she was forced to take tiny licks at the tasteless mud, choking down every last bit.

In the evening, Miss Potter would shut the window, cutting off the wind and the leaves and Mia's mom's apple scent. Then she would light a fire in the small cave, putting a flicker in Mr. Tod's eyes.

"Well, I'm *spent*," Miss Potter would say once the flames had faded to embers. "Good night, Little Miss! Sleep tight."

With that, she would slip into her room, and Mia would be left alone with the moon and the shadows and Mr. Tod's glowing gaze. When all was quiet, she would lick open the latch and lie by the door. And her mother would whisper soothing things through the cracks while Mia pretended not to hear the tears in her voice.

NINE

"Aaaaaaand finished!" Miss Potter sang out one evening.

She sat in front of Mia's cage. Only this time, she did not bring her pencil to skritch with. Instead, she brought several pages, which she tapped into a neat pile on her lap.

"This is only a rough draft, mind. I'm still working out the details." She studied the pages. "And I didn't quite get your eyes right, I'm afraid. You always look so *dour*."

She took a deep breath, then held up the first page. It showed a picture of Mia. Only, like the other watercolor animals, she stood on her hind paws. She carried a little nest filled with strawberries and wore a fluffy dress like the ones Miss Potter wore. A soft white something covered her head, save her ears, which stuck out the top.

Miss Potter cleared her throat and spoke in a pinched voice. "In the northlands, there was a valley of fog most white, with the golden tops of trees poking through. And in those trees lived a young fox kit. Her name was *Little Miss*."

Mia tried folding her paws over her ears, but they kept springing up. Had the fox with the glowing eyes listened to *The Tale of Mr. Tod*? Was this the last thing he ever did?

Miss Potter proceeded to tell the tale of a young vixen, whose two naughty brothers were always getting into trouble. After the brothers snuck onto a farm to hassle some chickens, the angry old farmer swore to shoot off their tails.

The words stirred something in Mia, and she tilted an ear.

The clever Little Miss managed to convince the farmer that the blood on her brothers' muzzles was nothing more than strawberry jam. In the end, the farmer left, scratching his head, and the fox kits made it home in time for their parents to lick their cheeks good night.

"The *end*," Miss Potter said, turning over the last page. She bared her teeth at Mia.

"And *now*, Little Miss, you shall live forever — in the hearts and minds of children *everywhere*."

Mia sniffed at the pages. Maybe living in the watercolor world wouldn't be so bad. She could remain in a story where she saved her siblings from the evils of the world until the end of time. Just as she feared she'd failed to do in the Eavey Wood.

"Well?" Miss Potter said. "What did you think? It may not be as exciting as the old tales with Peter, but *I* enjoy it. And to think we turned a tricksy fox into a hero!" She wrinkled her nose in that way Mia had come to learn wasn't a snarl. "I think someone deserves a treat."

She went to the kitchen and then brought back a raw piece of meat, which she tossed into the cage. Mia stared at it. Did this belong to the rabbit?

"Well?" Miss Potter said. "Go on, then."

Mia sniffed at the meat. She didn't touch it.

"Grown used to my oatmeal, have you?" Miss Potter said. "*Good.* Hunters are such nasty characters." She removed the meat and sighed. "Well ... no use in avoiding the inevitable."

She collected the cloth and the jar and the silver claw, blowing away the pencil dust. Then she reached for the skin tree, paused, and frowned around the room.

"Now where have my gloves run off to?"

She disappeared into her bedroom.

Mia licked open the cage's latch and bounded to the door. "Mom!" she howled. "You have to save me! She's going to do it right now!"

A moment later, her mom scratched at the door. "What can I do? I don't know what to do!"

Mia whimpered. Her mom was supposed to have all the answers. Mia searched the house, thinking. The window was too high. The door was blocked. Miss Potter had taken the sleeping liquid with her ... Then she saw the answer.

A minute later, Miss Potter swept back into the room, pulling on her gloves. "I heard your whimpering, Little Miss, and I am sorry about this. But there's no use in making it any more difficult than it already is."

When she turned around, Mia was back in her cage. Miss Potter poured the sleeping liquid over the cloth and then opened the cage with a gloved hand. Mia tried to leap out, but the woman caught her by the scruff, making Mia's spine bend and her paws dangle helplessly.

Miss Potter frowned. "Just know that I'm no happier about it than you are."

She pressed the cloth over Mia's muzzle and looked away. The woozy scent shot up Mia's nose. Her eyes watered over. The walls started to melt and bend.

Just before everything fell to darkness, the smell was gone.

"What's this?" Miss Potter said in a high-pitched voice.

She dropped Mia, half-conscious, back in her cage and closed it. Mia was barely able to keep her heavy eyelids open, but she watched through blurry lashes as Miss Potter went to her desk and picked up a drawing of Little Miss. A stream of pee trickled off it, smearing the pencil work.

"What happened?" Miss Potter said, horrified.

She searched the room for the culprit, never dreaming that Mia could have let herself out of her cage and then put herself back.

Mia wanted to howl to her mom, to let her know that she was still alive. But she could barely stay awake. Her head felt full of stones. She couldn't feel her paws. Her eyelids kept drifting shut without her permission.

Miss Potter let out a frustrated sound as she crumpled the paper and threw it in the trash.

"Well," she said, cleaning her hands in the small waterfall and then violently flicking droplets from her fingers. "I suppose we'll have to start over tomorrow." She went to the light switch and scowled at Mia's cage. "Get a good night's sleep, Little Miss. And *do* try not to look so dour in the morning."

She flicked off the light and then disappeared into her room.

There was a scratching at the door.

"Mia?" her mom howled. "Are you there? What did she do to you?"

Mia tried to swim out of sleep. But the walls couldn't hold their shape. The silver sticks wavered in and out of focus. Her eyes fell shut again.

"Mia!" her mom said, scratching.

Mia jerked awake. She needed to lick open the latch. She needed to let her mom know she was still alive. But she couldn't lift her head. Her tongue hung heavy in her mouth.

"Mia, please answer me!"

As the half-moon fell behind the trees, Mia's mom began to sob. Her mom couldn't smell her. Couldn't hear her. She thought Mia was nothing more than skin and pencil etchings.

After a long silence, her mom scratched at the door one last time. "I love you, Mia."

And Mia could do nothing except lie and listen as her mom said a tearful, howling goodbye, and then hopped off into the night.

Mia's heart beat too slow to break.

That night, Mia had a watercolor nightmare.

She stood in the Eavey Wood on her hind paws, holding a nest of peaches and centipedes. She was looking for her siblings

154

so she could feed them. A yelp echoed through the wood as Roa sprinted through the brambles, trying to escape the gooey-eyed Miss Vix.

Mia wanted to help her brother, but her paws wouldn't move. Even her whiskers refused to twitch. All she could do was stand and watch as Roa ran for his life, her teeth bared in a frozen smile.

TEN

"What a lovely morning!" Miss Potter said, bursting into the room the next day.

Mia lay in her cage. Her head was still woozy from the sleeping cloth, but it was her broken heart that kept her from getting up. Her mom had left her for dead.

"I was thinking, Little Miss," Miss Potter said, whisking around the room, collecting her pencil and paper. "Because we have to start over again, this might be the perfect opportunity to really get the story *right*. To return to the good old days when my books were urgent and frightening and sold like hotcakes."

Mia didn't budge. Maybe her mom had been right to leave her. Mia may have saved herself a few days by peeing on those pictures, but she still couldn't open the front door.

Miss Potter grabbed the silver claw and sharpened a pencil. "We'll get back to 'once upon a time' and 'happily ever after.' Why, this latest project has the potential to be even more popular than Peter ..."

Her face crumpled. She dropped the pencil and the silver claw and then hid in her hands. Her body shuddered with sobs, and she collapsed into a chair. Mia was so startled she sat upright.

Miss Potter recovered with a sniff. Her eyes glistened as she spun a circle of silver around her finger. "Who am I kidding? I gave up on happily ever after when my Mr. Warne died ..." Her breath caught. "Oh, Norman."

She dabbed at her face, smearing the blueberry tint from her eyes and smudging the red on her lips. Mia smelled the woman's salty tears and wondered if she, too, had lost her den.

Miss Potter ran her finger along Mia's cage. "Perhaps you miss someone too, hmm?" She sniffed. "That fox I caught before you? Some would say that's a ridiculous notion — that animals don't have feelings. And yet ..."

Miss Vix had warned Mia and her siblings that meeting eyes with another animal would result in a fight, be it with a sibling or a badger. But staring into Miss Potter's eyes made Mia's heart thump with something other than fear. This human seemed as sad as she was.

Keeping Mia's gaze, Miss Potter slowly slid her fingers through the silver sticks of the cage. Mia's paw lifted to move, but then came to rest again. The woman's fingers glided on either side of Mia's ear and then softly came together. The touch sent a trickle of warmth from her ear right to the hairless tip of her tail.

"Perhaps I'll make you my pet," Miss Potter whispered. "Would you like that? We could keep each other company during the long nights."

Mia delicately parted her teeth and gave the woman's fingers a lick. Her skin tasted of milk.

Miss Potter smiled sadly. "I think I know something that will cheer us both up."

She lifted the latch and opened the cage. Mia's ears perked. Was Miss Potter going to let her go? Mia's mom might still be nearby. She could still catch her apple scent. Her paws kneaded the cage, uncertain of whether to jump out or not.

Miss Potter went to her bedroom and then returned ... with a white cloth. Mia pressed into the back of her cage, whimpering.

"No need for that, Little Miss," Miss Potter said. "It's just a bonnet. Do you know what a bonnet is?"

Mia didn't. The rabbit had never mentioned it. She didn't dare sniff at the thing, in case it stole her breath again.

"See?" Miss Potter said, poking her fingers through two slits in the cloth. "These are for your ears. Now hold still ..."

She pressed the cloth close, and Mia turned her nose away, a growl building in her throat.

"Oh, come now," Miss Potter said. "You and I are getting along so well. Besides, it gets drafty in this old house at night. This will keep the warmth in. And you'll look *quite* handsome!"

The cloth came closer still, nearly reaching Mia's muzzle. Thoughts overwhelmed her. Miss Potter had changed her mind. She would clamp the cloth over Mia's nose, and Mia's legs would kick and kick until they fell limp and never kicked again. Then Miss Potter would scoop out her insides and replace her eyes with stones, and she'd wake up in a watercolor nightmare, where she'd never see her mom or her real siblings again.

"That's it," Miss Potter said, pressing the cloth closer.

Mia lashed, her fangs tearing through Miss Potter's delicate skin.

"EEEEEEEEEEEEEEEEE!"

The woman stumbled backward, blood streaming down her arm. Mia leapt out of the cage and sprinted to the front door, scratching at it, trying to get it to open.

"Mom! Mom!" she cried. "I'm here! I'm alive! Come back!"

Mia sensed something behind her ears and ducked, right before Miss Potter could grab her. She slipped through the woman's skirts and ran into the kitchen. Mia saw the brown jar on the counter. Before Miss Potter could reach it, Mia leapt, knocking the jar with her paws, sending it shattering across the floor.

The scent flooded the house, making Mia's head heavy, her paws start to drag. A hand seized her by the ears. She was yanked painfully upward, yowling over and over again until she was hurled back into her cage. The latch snapped shut.

Miss Potter hacked and coughed and waved her hand as she mopped up the spilled liquid. When the last of it was down the sink, she looked at the blood streaming down her arm. She turned and stared at Mia. The woman wore a new face now. Her skin twisted on her skull. The red on her lips was smeared. Her hair hung like dead weeds.

"I see," Miss Potter said in a dark voice. She went to her desk and grabbed Little Miss's surviving pages, smearing them with blood. "I should never have trusted a predator. Nasty, *nasty* things." She grabbed a match. "I refuse to lead my young readers astray."

She lit the match and touched its flame to the pages, making them crackle and burn bright. The pictures of Little Miss curled and blackened and then ended in ash. Miss Potter tossed the burning pages into the sink and opened the front door.

"I'll be back with more ether," she said, and then slammed the door shut.

Mia whimpered. She could still taste the woman's blood on her teeth.

ELEVEN

The sky was still blue when the moon rose pale and full in the window.

Now that Mia's pages were burned, where would she end up? She imagined her empty skin wandering lonely through the forest, searching for her mom. The skin had no eyes to see. It had no tongue to call out. When the skin remembered that it didn't have a heart to care whether it found its mom or not, it fell to the ground and never got up again.

Mia stared through the top of her cage at Mr. Tod.

"How do I get out of here?" she whispered.

The fox's eyes glowed with dusk. Mia followed his gaze to the rack where Miss Potter hung her extra skins. What could Mia do with that? She looked back to the fox, and her heart skipped a beat. Had his

163

muzzle turned? Or were the shadows playing tricks? Mr. Tod's eyes seemed to be pointed slightly to the left now. She followed his gaze to the stove.

"What are you trying to show me?" she asked, looking from the skin tree to the stove.

Mia remembered Miss Potter squawking like a bird after she'd accidentally dropped the match on the floor. The woman may have been able to make fire, but she still feared it. And when the flame leapt where it didn't belong, she had opened the door to let the smoke out ...

Mia's whiskers ticked up.

"Thank you," she whispered to the fox.

She licked open the latch.

The front door creaked open, and Miss Potter stepped inside, closing it behind her.

"They were out of ether," she said. "We'll have to do this the unpleasant way, I suppose."

Mia drew her muzzle back into the shadows under the skin tree. Her back was nestled beneath its arched roots. She waited.

There came the hiss of gas, the strike of a match, and a whoosh of flames. Next came the waterfall filling the pot. Then the sharpening of the silver claw — *shink shink shink!*

Mia peeked beneath the coats as Miss Potter approached her cage. The woman gasped when she found it empty.

"Little Miss?" Miss Potter said. Her steps grew more careful. *"Little Miss!"*

As soon as Miss Potter's toes were pointed away, Mia aimed her nose toward the firelit stove and pushed up on her hind legs, pressing her back into the arched roots of the skin tree.

The rack barely budged.

Miss Potter huffed. "Where has that little devil got off to?"

Mia pressed up again. The rack lifted momentarily, and the skins swayed toward the stove, but then the whole thing rocked back, painfully squishing her tail. Mia stifled a yelp.

"Come out, come out, wherever you are," Miss Potter sang, brandishing the silver claw and circling the room.

The skin tree teetered back and forth. When it tipped toward the stove again, Mia pushed up with everything she had, and the tree finally toppled, its skins falling with it. The top of the tree knocked the pot from the stove, and the skins landed on the flames. They started to smoke.

"My coats!" Miss Potter screamed. She ran and swept the smoldering skins off the stove, stomping out the fire.

A great cloud of smoke billowed to the ceiling, darkening the room. It stung Mia's eyes and tickled her lungs, but the smell filled her with hope.

The fire extinguished, Miss Potter ran, coughing, toward the front door. Mia followed like a shadow, careful to keep clear of the silver claw in the woman's hand. When the door flew open, Mia shot under the woman's skirts and between her feet toward freedom. Her tail brushed Miss Potter's ankle, and the woman screamed. A toe struck Mia's muzzle. A heel stabbed her tail. Everything became a tangle of legs and skirts and shrieks.

Mia managed to slip out into the open but found she was still inside. Her nose was no longer pointed toward the door.

"Rrraaaa!" Miss Potter screamed.

There came a whistling through the air, and Mia bounded away just before the silver claw could slice off her ear. She slipped into the first shadow she could find and cowered.

"Where did you go?" Miss Potter hissed.

In the shadows, Mia caught her breath. She'd been so close. But now Miss Potter was between her and the door. If she tried to escape, the woman would swing the silver claw, and that would be that for Mia.

"I believe that little devil purposefully set my kitchen on fire!" Miss Potter stalked around the room, snarling to herself. "Now, *where is she*?"

Mia watched the woman's heels stab around the room. She hoped with every beat of her heart for a clear path to the open door. Miss Potter kicked furniture, flipped over chairs, and whipped a tablecloth to the floor, huffing, searching. Mia cowered as Miss Potter bent at the hips with a grunt, peering under the sink, the table, the cabinet.

"Aha!" she said, crouching near the bookcase. *"Found you!"*

She seized the tail that stuck out from the shadows and gave it a tug. Before Miss Potter realized she was pulling on Mr. Tod's tail, Mia bounded toward the open door. But just as she was about to leap outside, her nose smooshed against something soft, something invisible, and it bounced her backward.

Mia stared in shock. There was nothing in the doorway. But she couldn't pass through it. Had Miss Potter already trapped her in a story? Had Mia struck the border of the page?

"Thank goodness," Miss Potter said, tossing Mr. Tod aside. "The screen caught you."

Screen? Mia squinted at the entrance, and she saw the silver sticks, as tiny as hairs, making squares the size of bugs' eyes. Her heart sank. Miss Vix had warned her. For all of Mia's trickery, humans were cleverer by a landslide.

A sharp heel stomped on Mia's tail. Her yelp was cut short when a rope slipped around her throat, jerking her upward until she dangled before the naked face of Miss Potter.

"*Monstrous* thing," the woman spat.

Mia's eyes watered. Her legs twitched helplessly. She couldn't breathe.

Miss Potter kicked open the screen and hauled Mia, dangling by her neck, outside.

"I never should have trusted a fox," the woman said.

She tossed the rope's end around a stick that stuck out from the den's side, just like the one that held the rabbit's skin.

Mia stopped struggling as the lights in her eyes began to fade. Her last thought before everything went dark was that she didn't even get to say goodbye to her siblings.

SOMEWHERE IN THE Antler Wood, leaves rattled without wind.

The little one shifted her paws, making sure her skin was still on tight.

No such thing as stealing eyes, she told herself. *No such thing as tree-tall things with no fur. No such thing as watercolor nightmares.*

"Wait," the beta said. "Is Mia okay? She didn't … *die*, did she?"

"Patience," the storyteller said.

The little one was really starting to hate that word.

"Hey … ," the third kit said to the fifth. "*Your* fur's pretty soft. I wonder if Miss Potter will come humming for you tonight?"

A shiver whipped the fifth kit, Mars, right up to his paws.

"I'm hungry," he said. He curled his tongue, trying a yawn. "I mean sleepy. G'night!"

He waddled toward home. The third one grinned and stepped on a branch, snapping it. The sound startled Mars, who sprinted, leapt over a log, and then belly flopped in a bed of lilies.

The alpha chuckled. "Good one."

Four little foxes.

"We're ready for the next part," the beta said.

"More than ready," the third said.

The little one wanted to follow Mars, all the way home. But she had to find out what happened to Mia. She just had to. She lay on her paws so they wouldn't be tempted to run.

"We return to the Boulder Fields," the storyteller said. "To the forest's edge, where Uly has been sitting, waiting for his mother to come and collect him …"

CREEEAAAK
THUMP!
CREEEAAAK
THUMP!

ONE

Uly wasn't eaten in his first hour in the forest. Nor in his second.

He sat only a few tails into the trees, foreleg folded under his chest, trying to remain inconspicuous. He watched as the rocky shadow of the Great Boulder slid from one side of the canopy to the other, certain that at any moment, his mom was going to poke her nose into the forest, having chased Mr. Scratch away. She loved Uly too much to leave him all alone.

She would come for him. Any moment now ...

With night came a steady wind that lashed the trees and shifted the moonlight. The shadows began to play tricks on Uly's eyes. The leaves overhead became the ruffled wings of bats. The bush to his right was the

175

bristled back of a bear. And to his left was a tree of moaning faces.

Uly covered his eyes with his good forepaw. It didn't help. He could still hear the rustling trees, still see terrifying images on the backs of his eyelids. He decided it was probably a good idea *not* to wait for his mom any longer and instead to exit the forest as quickly as foxingly possible. He hopped toward the mouth of the wood, where he'd entered.

But then a hooting turned him left. A bone snap spun him right. And a sound like slopping entrails swung him around again. Suddenly, Uly didn't know which way was straight ahead. The branches of the forest pointed every direction, making him feel cross-eyed. Everything was shadows and more shadows.

"Mom?" he whispered.

He swiveled his ears, listening for the familiar sounds of the Boulder Fields, but all he heard was the creaking of trees. He sniffed for familiar scents, but the air was barky and strangled. He wanted to howl for his mom to come and save him, but the forest was filled with ears and bellies, searching for a snack.

Uly sniffed out a nook in the roots of a tree, where nothing could sneak up behind him, and he wrapped his tail around himself.

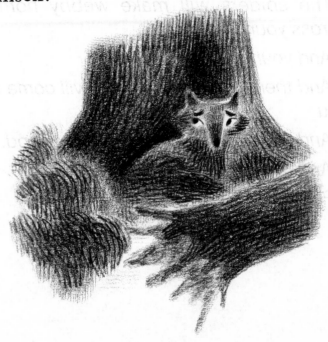

Ever since he could remember, Uly's sisters had told him he wouldn't survive kithood. He couldn't jump. Couldn't hunt. He couldn't even clean himself without falling over.

He could almost hear them now, whispering in the dark forest.

Don't worry, Ewwly.

Once you're dead, you can still make friends.

The centipedes'll twine through your nostrils

And out your ears.

The spiders will make webby homes across your rib cage

And your eye sockets.

And then the Shrouded Fox will come for you

And steal you away to the Underwood.

And that's where you'll live

Forever.

TWO

A groan startled Uly awake.

He tumbled out of the hairy roots with a yelp, certain he was about to be plucked up by a branchy claw and devoured by the tree with many faces. When nothing grabbed him, he blinked open his eyes. Patches of golden light writhed on the forest floor.

Morning had come. He hadn't been so sure it would.

The groan sounded again, and Uly realized it was coming from his own stomach. He hadn't eaten a thing since that baby squirrel. Mud clung to his fur, and his skin clung to his ribs. He remembered his mother's warming words. Maybe he was so skinny that no hunters would want to eat him.

He sniffed the morning air for her scent. Nothing.

His stomach grumbled again. He had to eat something. Soon. He marked the roots of the tree so his mom could find him. Then he took a deep breath.

"Come on, paws."

And for the first time, Uly set off to hunt for himself.

"The forest is a feast," Uly said aloud in a reassuring sort of way. "And foxes are clever, above all, above all."

Unfortunately, neither statement brought any squirrel babies tumbling from the treetops.

He searched his memory for the hunting lessons his mother had taught his sisters:

Listen for rustlings and gnawings in the brush.

Stalk quietly until your prey flees into the open.

Match your movement with its movement.

Low muzzle for a bird or squirrel. High muzzle for a mouse.

Bound from afar.

That last part didn't really work for a fox with three legs. Uly wouldn't be able to bound over a fire ant if a whole heap of mouse guts was waiting for him on the other side.

He swiveled his ears, listening with one and then the other. The forest was filled with scrabbles and nibbles and tiny digging paws. The delicious sounds skittered through his muzzle, curling his lips. How could he catch them? Prey lived high in the trees or buried deep in the ground, guarded by burrs and thorns and bugs that would bite his eyelids.

He tried sniffing out a stream of scent along the forest floor, just like his mom had taught him. He sniffed and sniffed until his nose grew so dry he was afraid it might crumble off.

It was no use. All he smelled was dirt and leaf mulch.

He plopped down again, ready to give up and make everlasting pals with the centipedes.

"Tasty hiding! Tasty hiding!"

Uly perked his ears.

"Tasty hiding! Tasty hiding!"

A bird sang in the treetops. Uly had spent so much time alone in the den's entrance while his sisters fought one another that he had come to understand many birdsongs. He'd listen to the birds sing and then watch as they swooped up some delicious morsel.

"Tasty hiding! Tasty hiding!"

He sniffed in the direction where the bird's bill was pointed. A coppery scent laced the wind, leading him to a split in a tree trunk. His stomach gurgled. He licked his whiskers. There were warm things in there. And they were moving.

Uly crouched behind a shrub. Unless his nose was lying, the critters inside that trunk were small and helpless and wouldn't be able to put up a fight. He bent low on his foreleg and wiggled his hips in a way he'd seen his sisters do a hundred times before. He made a mighty bound toward the tree, his forepaw thumping along the ground.

He hadn't smelled the mother possum. She scurried down the trunk and into the split, reappearing a moment later with three baby possums dangling from her mouth. She flashed Uly a murderous look and then scampered away.

Uly was so upset that he fell over. His stomach whined as several other edible critters fled the area, running from the kit whose pawsteps were as loud as crashing boulders.

THREE

Evening fell again. Branches chewed the
sky. Uly lay, head in the dirt, blinking dully.
His stomach had stopped growling — as if
even it had given up on him.

Ever since he was a tiny kit, Uly had
known he would spend his life alone.
He'd never meet a vixen. Never start a
den. He'd starve somewhere all by himself.
He'd just never thought that day would
come this soon.

He closed his eyes and waited for the
spiders and centipedes to make a home
out of him.

Snff snff.

A scent caught him by the nostrils.

Snff snff snfffff.

It was so strong and succulent that it
rolled him up onto his stomach. This was
not the smell of just-born bodies, furless

and helpless and ready for eating. It was *warmer*.

Uly got to his paws and followed the scent. He had smelled fire once before when the firs had smoldered in the distance, casting a smoky shadow over the Boulder Fields. He had smelled entrails, steaming in the open air when his sisters ripped open a groundhog. But this intoxicating scent lay somewhere in between, singeing his nostrils as much as it enticed them.

Snfffff.

The smell twined between the leaves, tickling Uly's nose and pulling him along. It got his stomach rumbling again, and drips of drool pattered the dirt.

Snff snff snff.

Soon the scent was all around him, so thick it was almost filling. The air became hazy, and he saw coils of smoke twine through a clearing. Uly froze. No birds sang. No mice bounded through the elder trees. As if the creatures knew to keep quiet in this place.

But then …

Creeeaaak THUMP! Creeeaaak THUMP!

185

He crouched low. His sisters had never told him stories like this before. What smelled this enticing but sounded so strange?

Creeeaaak THUMP! Creeeaaak THUMP!

He glanced back into the tangled forest and the starvation that awaited him there. Then, as quietly as possible, he hopped toward the clearing, moving from tree to tree. He peeked around a trunk and was so confused by what he saw that he had to blink a few times.

The thing in the clearing was as big as a boulder and half as tall as the trees. Its sides were perfectly flat, save the top, which was sloped with dead grass. Something like a rocky trunk stuck out of the grass, spewing the delicious-smelling smoke. In the boulder's side was a hole, flickering bright as a firefly. It cast a yellow haze through the dying dusk light.

Uly quirked his head. This boulder was hollow. And something was living inside it.

Creeeaaak THUMP! Creeeaaak THUMP!

The sound was coming from the far side of the hollow boulder.

Uly licked his lips. His pounding heart and grumbling stomach played tug-of-war inside him. His stomach whined.

"Okay, okay," Uly whispered. "I get it. Shh."

Keeping low, he hopped into the clearing, whiskers alert. He sniffed along the boulder's flat side, rounding the first corner. Flies buzzed around a pile of something dark and wet. Uly hopped closer and found entrails. Rotting entrails, just sitting in the grass. Above them, the skin of a rabbit dangled from a stick — as if it had snagged its ears on a branch and spilled its guts out.

Creeeaaak THUMP!

The sound wasn't coming from the rabbit.

Uly left the entrails and slowly peeked around the next corner.

Creeeaaak THUMP!

His heart went cold. It was the skin of a little girl fox — dangling just like the rabbit's. She hung from her muzzle by what looked like a vine. Her body swung back and forth, her hind legs striking the side of the hollow boulder.

187

Creeeaaak THUMP! Creeeaaak THUMP!

Uly backed away. The boulder must be a trap for foxes. Any moment, a vine was going to swoop down, snag him by the muzzle, and —

He nearly jumped out of his skin when the fox opened her mouth and dropped to the ground. He froze as he tried to make sense of what he was seeing. The fox was more than just skin. And she hadn't been hanging from the vine at all. She'd been tugging at it. It was still wrapped around her neck.

The girl fox stared at Uly, wide-eyed. He stared back, holding perfectly still, hoping she hadn't seen him in the low flickering light.

"Are you" — she said — "*stuffed?*"

"HIC!"

Uly ran from the clearing — forepaw slipping, chest thumping — scrambling along the grass until he leapt into a bush, where he froze and held his breath.

"Hello?" the girl fox called. *"Hello?"*

Uly crouched in the bush. Not all foxes were nice, he knew. Not even if they were related to you. And foxes who weren't

188

related to you could be even worse. *Territorial.* That was the word. If he went back out there, the fox might seize him by the throat and shake him to death.

"Are you still there?" the girl fox said.

Uly's stomach whined. Then again, if he grew any hungrier, he might vanish with a small pop. Maybe this fox would share some of those entrails. He'd even take the chewy bits.

"Um, yes — *hic!*" he called out. "I'm here." Hearing the sound of his own pathetic voice made him wince. So he said, growlier, *"And me. There's two of us."*

This was the brave voice that made his mom laugh. He hoped it sounded menacing now.

"And you can't hurt us!" he said. Then, growling, *"Because we'll chomp you to pieces."*

The fox in the clearing was quiet a moment. "I don't want to fight you."

"You're right," he responded. "You don't. Because my claws are as sharp as — *hic* — slivers." Then, *"And my teeth are as long as icicles. They'll freeze you and you'll shatter into a mi—* hic *—illion pieces."*

189

The voice in the clearing fell silent. "Guess I shouldn't mess with you, then."

Uly's jaw fell open. The scary voice had worked. No one had ever believed he could hurt them before. His sisters used to tease that he was so harmless mice camped in his mouth at night. This fox hadn't so much as snickered at him.

"Will … will you help me?" she said. "I got caught by a human, and I lost my mom, and now the human's gonna boil me up and stick me in a page, and I'm — I'm *stuck*."

Uly's ears pricked. He didn't know what a *hue-mun* was, or what boiling was — in fact, he hadn't understood most of the sentence. Only that this fox had lost her mom. He was about to tell her he'd lost his mom too when he caught himself. You didn't get tricked by your sisters a thousand and one times without learning a thing or two.

He remembered how the fox had swung by her muzzle from that vine, and his ears folded back. "How do I — er, how do we know you aren't a dead fox who's gonna gobble us up?" Then, growlier, *"Yeah — hic — how do we know that?"*

The fox huffed, frustrated. "'Cause dead foxes can't talk, *duh!*"

She had a point.

Then again, this fox had been dangling one minute, and the next, she was on her paws.

"How do we know you aren't lying?"

"I can't prove to you that I'm not dead other than by talking to you!" the fox said. "Besides, *you're* the one who's lying!"

"Wh-what do you mean?" Uly asked. *"Y-yeah, what do you mean?"*

The fox snorted. "Hiccups aren't contagious!"

A stone turned over in Uly's stomach when he realized how he'd given away that he was just one fox instead of two. "*Hic!* Um, uh, I gotta — *hic* — go," he said, hobbling away. "Um, I mean *we've* gotta go. *Yeah, good luck with* — hic — *with everything* — hic!"

"No, wait!" the fox called out. "Please don't leave! I'm sorry I called you a liar. I'm sorry I said 'duh.' I'm going to die here! Miss Potter's going to kill me! The water is boiling, and she'll be back any second, and — and — and — *please!*"

Uly stopped. "What's stuck you?"

"A rope," the fox said.

Rope? Uly peeked into the clearing. From high on the boulder grew the brown vine that wrapped around the fox's neck. *So she'd been trying to free herself…*

The fox's eyes pierced through the dusk. She looked softer than Uly's sisters. Chubbier. Her fur smelled of unripe apples.

"If I help you," Uly said, "can I eat those innards?"

"Yes!" the fox said. "They're all yours! Just hurry!"

Uly hopped a few tails into the clearing. By the flickering light of the hollow boulder, he got a good look at the fox. Her fur was as light as pollen, with gray stars sprinkled through her coat. She was a little pudgy — something Uly didn't even know was possible for a fox — and the tip of her tail was hairless.

"Can you" — the fox craned her head, trying to nibble at the vine around her neck — "help me get this thing off?"

Uly's first thought was, *No. No, he couldn't.* No one had ever asked him for help before, because — well, he wasn't good at things. Now and then, his sisters had used his back as a boost to get on top of a rock that they never invited him on. But beyond that, he wasn't any help at all.

The fox stared at him with her blue-swirl eyes. "I'm not gonna hurt you."

Uly still didn't move. He wasn't so worried about that anymore. Just of making a fool of himself.

"You have your friend to keep you safe, right?" the girl fox said. She roughened her voice. *"The one who sounds like this?"*

"Oh, right, yeah," he said, searching out a believable place his fake friend could hide. "He climbed a tree. He can drop from above like rain made of teeth."

"Fang rain." The fox nodded. "Got it."

Uly hopped forward, head low. "What do I do?"

The fox took the vine in her mouth and gave it a tug. "It squeezes my neck whenever I pull on it. I need you to hold it still so I can slip out."

Uly did what he was told. He took the hairy vine in his teeth and pulled. The fox wiggled and jerked her neck.

"Pull!" she said.

"Ah'm twying!" he said, mouth full.

"Come on! Pull! Pull!"

"Ah'm twying! Ah'm twying!"

And then the vine fell loose in his mouth, and the fox was free.

"Run!" she cried. "Forget the entrails!"

She darted into the wood, leaving Uly with the rope. He dropped it with a *thunk*.

"Um?" he said.

A section of the hollow boulder smacked open, and something screamed in a high-pitched shrill. *"Gobs and naping! Sheez froke thuh ropplin!"*

The creature had wild gray hair that stuck out at all angles and a loose skin that swept all the way around two knobby knees … Uly's heart nearly stopped when he saw that the thing walked on its hind legs. Its forelegs hung high on its body. And instead of claws, it had long fleshy appendages that wriggled like fat worms.

"Fye!" the wild thing screeched. *"Pather!"*

Uly bolted after the girl fox. And even on only three legs, he was too quick for the creature with two.

194

FOUR

Uly came to a stop in a grove of birch trees. Panting, he looked back to make sure the horror on two legs wasn't still following him. The forest was still.

"Um ... fox?" he called quietly. "Ch-chubby fox?"

No response.

He sniffed the air. Now that the haze of smoke was gone, he was able to pick up the fox's unripe-apple scent. He followed it to a puddle and found her staring at her own reflection. She didn't look up when he approached.

He hopped closer, sniffing warily. "What are you doing?"

The fox's head snapped up, and she came at him in a flash. He squeezed his eyes shut, waiting for her teeth to sink into his throat. When he felt nothing, he cracked an eyelid and found her face pressed close to his.

"What color are my eyes?" she said.

"They're" — he gulped — "gold. Blue and gold."

The fox nodded. She returned to the puddle and again stared at her rippling reflection. She seemed surprised by the fox staring back at her.

"Um," Uly said, "what's your name?"

She kept staring at the puddle.

"Mine's Uly."

The only response was a loon in the distance.

Finally, the girl fox took a breath. "I was in there so long I thought I'd missed it."

"Missed what?"

"My kithood." The fox stared at her reflection and blew out her cheeks. "I got kinda chubby, huh?"

"I don't know. I ... didn't know you before."

She sighed. "I guess it doesn't matter." She quirked an eyebrow. "I'm *free*." She took off, darting this way then that, weaving through the trees. "It feels so good to be *out*! My legs are all long and … *springy*! Ha ha!"

She zoomed circles around Uly, growling and making little nips at his ears and tail.

He cowered. "Wh-what are you doing?"

"Making up for lost *time*!"

Uly ducked as she bounded over his back and then bounded over it again.

"Are you being mean?" he said, ears flattened.

"No! Playful!"

He tried to stand upright just as the fox's paws landed on his back. She performed a fancy kickflip, sending his body thumping to the ground.

"Ow!" he cried.

"Oops!" she said, giggling. "Sorry!" And she took off running again.

Uly did not like this fox's playfulness. Not one bit. He would have thought twice about helping her escape from that vine if he'd known she was going to act like this.

He started to hop into the forest.

"Hey!" the girl fox called after him. "Where ya goin'?"

"Er, nowhere?" Uly said, sitting back down. "Please don't jump on me again."

"I'm Mia," she said, tail wagging.

Uly nodded slowly. "I'm still Uly."

He wondered what Mia saw when she looked at him. He was small for his moons, he knew, and it was hard not to notice his withered front paw. His legs were as skinny as sticks, and his fur was ragged from too much scratching. His mom had told him he had a violet tinge to his fur, like he'd been "smooched all over by a blackberry bush." But his sisters teased him that his eyes were always wet and shiny, like he was about to cry any moment.

Uly widened his eyes, drying them out so Mia wouldn't think he was scared.

"Nice to meet you, Uly!" she said, not seeming to notice his paw or his fur or his eyes or anything. She got low on her fore-legs and wiggled her hips. "What should we do?"

Uly's stomach pinched and let out a gurgle.

"Um," he said, wavering. "A-a-a-are you hungry at all?"

"Nope!" Mia said. She did a spin. "But let's hunt something!"

His stomach whined again. "Um, yeah. Okay."

"Oh," Mia said, seeing his withered paw for the first time. "What happened?"

"What, this?" Uly sniffed at it like it was no big deal. "It's always been like this."

"Huh." She stared at his paw with a sadness in her eyes, as if it reminded her of something. But then she shook the thought away. "Welp, see ya!"

Mia gave her hips another wiggle and then darted off between the trees. Uly sat and waited. He'd grown very good at it. He listened to the insects and the birds and the wind in the leaves, trying to ignore his grumbling stomach.

He'd thought maybe Mia had abandoned him forever when he heard a splash and a miserable croak, and then she came trotting back, fur dripping, a dead creature in her jaws. Uly had never seen anything like it before. It wasn't quite a frog, and it wasn't quite a lizard, and it had gills like a fish.

Mia laid the creature on the ground. "I've never hunted something by myself before!"

She pinned the creature's tail between her paws and ripped it in half, plopping the hind parts in front of him.

"What ... is it?" he said, trying not to wrinkle his muzzle.

"I don't know! It has gills, but it *walks around*! Ha ha." She snorted. "The forest is squipping crazy."

Uly's eyes went wide. A word like that would get his sisters' lips bitten. But Mia hadn't even batted an eyelash.

His stomach gurgled again. He bit into the creature, and a gush of slime squirted down his throat. At first, he fought not to gag, but then his teeth ripped through the flesh, and hunger roared up inside him. After that, he couldn't devour the legs quickly enough.

"This tastes *amazing*!" Mia said, gulping down an eyeball. "I've been eating hot mud for *weeks*!"

"Hot ... mud?" Uly said.

"Uh-huh!"

The two feasted in slobbery silence. Uly could feel his stomach stretching, his skin pushing away from his ribs. He had to stop himself from whimpering it felt so good to eat.

"Y'know," Mia said, licking slime from her beard, "just 'cause you're not a mouser doesn't mean you can't still catch stuff. You could use the nap-and-capture technique."

Uly stopped eating. "You can catch things by taking naps?"

"Yep! You just pretend you're dead. Like this." Mia flopped over on her side, letting her tongue hang out. "And when something delicious comes sniffing" — she leapt up, chomping her teeth and making Uly wince — "you kill it! Miss Vix told me about that trick."

Uly nodded. He might be able to actually try that. So long as he didn't start hiccupping.

"Why are you being so nice to me?" he asked.

"What do you mean?"

"I don't know," he said.

When the gill creature was nothing but bones, Mia got up, shook the slime from her beard, and then came at him, teeth bared.

"Wh-what are you doing?" he asked, pressing his muzzle protectively into his throat.

"I was going to clean you," Mia said, like it was the most obvious thing in the world. "We just ate."

"Oh," Uly said.

No one had ever wanted to clean him before. His mom did it only because his sisters refused. And she hadn't cleaned him since Ava died.

He swallowed. "Okay."

Mia gave his muzzle a lick. His forepaw trembled. A snarl rose in his throat. But as she started to clean his ears, he leaned into it. Her tongue was warm and scratchy, and sent shivers to the end of his tail. He widened his eyes again, trying to stop the tears.

Once Mia had finished cleaning, she said, "Does your friend need cleaning too?"

Uly shook himself out of his reverie. "Who?"

"Your" — Mia nodded toward the canopy — "friend?"

"Oh. Um … not right now. I cleaned him earlier."

She gave him a knowing smirk. Then she closed her eyes and jutted her muzzle forward.

Uly hesitated. "You want me to …"

Her ear twitched. "If you don't mind."

Anytime he'd tried to clean his sisters, they had bounded away, screaming, *"Yuck! Ewwly* breath!"

He gave Mia's ear a small lick. Then another. And another. Her fur tasted of smoke at first. Then something bland. But once he'd cleaned that away, she tasted as sweet and sour as unripe apples. Mia whimpered just like he had. As if she, too, hadn't been cleaned in a long time.

When he finished, Mia shook her ears dry.

"Welp," she said in a goodbye sort of way.

"Yeah," Uly said, heart skipping a beat. "Welp."

"I should get going," she said. "My mom's waiting for me on the other side of these trees. And I don't want her worrying about me."

"Oh, yeah," he said. "Me too. Er, I have to go find my friend … the one hiding in the trees. So we can go to where we're going, which is pretty close to here."

"Okay, then," she said.

"Okay."

His heart sank. Mia had nipped at him and jumped over him and knocked him over. But she had fed and cleaned him too. Uly knew that the moment she walked away it would feel like his guts were yanked out, leaving him as empty as that dangling rabbit skin.

He pointed his newly cleaned whiskers toward where he thought his mom might be. And he knew that he was wrong.

"Have fun with your friend!" Mia said.

"I — I will," Uly said. "Have fun with your mom."

She walked off slowly. "See ya!"

"See ya," he called after her.

"Bye!"

"Yeah, bye."

And Mia set off in one direction while Uly set off in the same direction, and they did not part ways again … for a time.

"**THAT ONE WASN'T** scary at all!" the third kit said. "Like, really truly!"

"Yeah," said the alpha. "That was almost … *heartwarming*."

"I liked it," the beta said.

"You would," the third one said.

The sky above the Antler Wood was greeny-white now.

The little one was relieved to hear a nice part of the story for once. But she could sense they were far from the end. The sounds of the Antler Wood still made her skin jumpy. Each tumbling leaf swiveled her ears. Every shadow looked like a dangling fox skin.

"Mia and Uly's meeting was a welcome respite from what they'd been through," the storyteller said. "But it's a dangerous thing to start caring for someone else. Now they each had two foxes to look after instead of one. And they were about to stumble upon a place that was neither field nor forest. Neither meadow nor wood. They were going to see something few foxes had seen before. And those who had seen it had not escaped with their lives."

If the little one had felt a touch of safety, that strangled it.

THE SLITHER
OUT OF
DARKNESS

ONE

Uly followed Mia's unripe-apple scent through the forest as she talked faster than a tree full of chickadees.

"So then my mom asked if Miss Vix bit me, and I said no, and then she asked if I was sure and made me drink water for some reason, and when I did, she told me I was the only kit who passed the stinky-yellow test. I think if Miss Vix *had* bitten my tail, then I would've failed, but because she only got a few hairs off the end, I *passed*. And that's why I got to leave the Eavey Wood when my brothers and sister didn't."

The branches were growing thicker. The canopy strangled the sky. Mia's words made the shadows come to life in Uly's eyes, with rickety heads and gooey eyes and dry fangs. He wanted to bite Mia's whiskers and tell her that being lost in the wood was no time for scary stories. But he didn't know her well enough.

"So then me and my mom came north," Mia continued, "and that's when things got *really* scary."

She proceeded to tell him about the furless terror who walked on two legs and trapped animals' essences in white leaves before ripping off their skins, replacing their eyes with shiny rocks, and stuffing them full of straw.

The story made the trees reach toward Uly with their long fingers. He hopped to catch up to Mia's tail — even though she was the one scaring him.

"And that's when you showed up and saved my life!" Mia said, peeking over her shoulder. "Did I say thanks? 'Cause, thanks."

"Oh, um," Uly said, "you're welcome."

He was still trying to figure this Mia kit out. He didn't understand why she insisted on hunting for him and cleaning him one moment, and then the next, nipping his ears or telling him a story so terrifying it made his eyes water. Was Mia more like his mom … or his sisters?

"*So!*" Mia spun around and trotted backward. "Two kits in the forest. Funny, right?"

"Um, sure," Uly said. "Funny."

"Why are *you* out here?" she asked.

"Well ..."

Uly had flashes of his father — his ashen face, his moon-bright fangs, his lips saying, *Break its neck.* He didn't want to tell Mia his story, because then she would know that his family thought he was as disposable as a gopher's toenails.

He cleared his throat. "I just, uh, went out hunting and got lost and" — he hopped over a pebble — "never found my way back."

"Huh," Mia said, eyes narrowing.

She turned right side around and continued through the heather. Uly worried that he'd given himself away. Any moment, Mia might start seeing him as dead weight she had to drag around.

He bounded to catch up. "I, um, think I could tell you what happened to your brothers and sister."

"What do you mean?" Mia said.

Uly's sisters had told him about the yellow stench once. They had tried to convince him their mother had it, and that she was going to eat him for supper.

"So, if the yellow gets inside you," he said, "then it, uh, strangles your personality, making it go away forever. Your tongue runs dry, and the only thing that will quench it is, well ... *blood*. You start hearing whispers in your head that tell you to kill, and your gooey eyes start seeing everything as food. Even other foxes. Once you bite someone and pass the yellow on to them, then you dry up and you die."

Mia stopped walking. She turned and stared at him.

Uly glanced around uncomfortably. "So, yeah, um, that's what it is."

She looked at him a long time. "You're a liar," she finally said. "My siblings are safe in the Eavey Wood. They're taking lessons from Miss Vix."

"Oh." Uly gulped. His ears flattened. "Yeah. Probably. Sorry."

She continued on in silence.

"Hey, um, you want me to clean your ears again?" he asked her.

"No," she said.

TWO

The breath of the trees grew damp, and the ground grew squishy underpaw. Mia and Uly found themselves walking through the dripping gray expanse of a swamp.

"What *is* this place?" he whispered.

"How should I know?" she said.

She'd barely spoken to him since he'd told her about the yellow. Now that it was quiet, he realized how much her voice had brightened their journey. Strange sounds echoed from the swamp's belly — *slurp*s and *slog*s and *sploosh*es and *croak*s.

Uly saw unsettling shapes in the darkness — spidery blossoms, green-crusted mushrooms, and moss that hung like long gray foxtails. He saw an insect dissolve crisply in the petals of a flower and a frog try to catch a wriggling worm hiding under a stone, only for the stone to snap shut, slicing the frog in two.

His ears folded. "Do you, um, know where you're going?"

"North," Mia said.

She stopped at the edge of a murky stretch that was half-grass, half-puddle. She sniffed at a row of dry humps and then hopped across them.

"Why north?" Uly asked, doing his best to follow, forepaw wobbling on each hump.

"My mom told me to go to the other side of the forest," she called back. "When we first got to the trees, the sun was setting to the *left*, so that would have been *west*. So as long as I keep the purple in my eyes, we'll head *north* out of the forest, and I'll find her."

"Oh, right," Uly said, like what she'd said made sense to him.

The humps soon came to an end, and the ground grew soppier still. With each step, Uly had to yank his forepaw out of the marsh and lunge forward, only for it to plunge deep again.

Yank. Hop. *Sploosh.*

Yank. Hop. *Sploosh.*

He tried to hop again, but the mud held tight to his forepaw, and his muzzle splashed into the water. He whimpered bubbles.

Mia didn't seem to notice, continuing without him.

"Wait!" he called.

She looked back and huffed, annoyed.

He couldn't lose her. She was the only reason he hadn't starved to death. He tried to pull his leg free, but white pain bloomed in his shoulder.

"I'm stuck," he said.

"You've just got a mild case of soppy paws," Mia called to him. "It'll pass once we get to dry land."

She kept walking, and Uly gazed the way they'd come. "Can't we just go back? It's easier back there."

"There's traps that way," she said. "And that's where Miss Potter lives. Besides" — she bounded twice through the water — "my mom's waiting for me."

He gave another tug on his leg, but it was stuck deep.

"Why do you want me to come with you anyway?" he asked.

"Because you saved me from getting boiled and eaten, *duh*," she said. "Now come *on*."

Uly hadn't meant to save her. He'd just been in the right place at the right time and done exactly what she told him to do. He wasn't heroic. Just lucky.

When he didn't budge, Mia pointed her nose into the dripping darkness and gave a deep sniff. "Mm! Do you *smell* that?"

He sniffed. All he could smell was drowned insects and fish leavings. "Smell what?"

"There are *centipedes*," she said. "And — *snff snff* — mm! *Peaches* past these trees."

"I know what you're trying to do," he said. "And it won't work." He looked down at his stuck leg. He didn't like being treated like a baby kit. "Besides, I don't even *like* peaches. They make my paw sticky."

He didn't mention that centipedes would probably make a home out of his eye sockets someday and that the thought of eating them gave him the creeps.

Mia scowled at him. "Why are you being so stubborn?"

216

He scowled back. *Because,* he wanted to tell her, *if I don't get dissolved by a flower or chomped by a rock, then my foreleg is gonna get yanked right out of its socket. Because if I try and take one more step through this water, I'm gonna pass out and drown. Because I don't know if you're more like my mom or my sisters ...*

Uly's whiskers perked. He had an idea.

"The *Golgathursh,*" he whispered darkly.

"The *huh?*"

He gazed into Mia's eyes. "The *Golgathursh.*"

"What the squip is a Gorga— a Gluga— a Gurgl—"

"Golgathursh."

"Yeah, that."

He licked his lips. He wanted to scare Mia out of heading north, scare her from dragging him deeper into the dripping mouth of the swamp. And the best way he knew to do that was with one of his sisters' scary stories.

"The Golgathursh lives in the bottom of every pond, every puddle," he began.

The first time Uly's mom had taken him and his sisters to the rain pool, carrying

217

them one by one across the crack, his sisters had pointed their noses toward the water's surface, where scaly backs slipped and shimmered.

See that, Uly? Ava had said.

That's the Golgathursh, said Ada.

Nuh-uh, Uly had said. *That's just* carp.

Nope, Ani said.

It's the Golgathursh, said Ali.

It lives in the bottom of every lake.

Every pond.

Every puddle.

The Golgathursh is bigger than boulders.

Bigger than mountains.

It has serpents for legs.

And a body made of mouths.

And nothing else.

If you step too close to the water's edge —

There'll be a sploosh —

And a snap —

And all of a sudden you'll be just half a fox —

Instead of a whole one.

Of course, Ava concluded, you'd be even less than half a fox, wouldn't you, Ewwly?

His sisters had snickered.

"That's crazy talk," Mia said. "No one's ever even heard of a *Googulthrosh* before."

"Golgathursh," Uly said.

He didn't believe in it either. But he couldn't let Mia know that. Not when he was trying to scare her.

"*Nothing* is made of just mouths," she said. "How would it *poop*? Now, come on."

Uly rested his chin in the water. *"No."*

Mia splashed back to him. She clamped onto his scruff and pulled.

"Come. *On!*" she said, mouth full of fur.

"No!" he said. "If we go any deeper, the Golgathursh is gonna eat us!"

"The Grogglethrish isn't even real!"

"It's *Golgathursh!*"

Mia gave a sharp yank, and her fangs sent a piercing pain through Uly's neck. Anger shot straight to the tips of his ears.

"You said the yellow wasn't real either! But it still killed your brothers and sister!"

Mia released his scruff. Her muzzle clamped shut.

Uly frowned, his neck still throbbing. He'd known what he'd said would hurt her. But he didn't care. She was hurting his foreleg by forcing him to walk through this marsh. She was hurting his scruff by tugging on it. She tortured him with scary stories while they were lost in a dark and dangerous place. She deserved it.

Mia's eyes wavered with tears. "Fine. Stay here and die. See if I care."

She bounded through the wet grass.

"Fine!" he called after her. "Maybe I will!"

Uly watched, scowling, until her tail faded to gray and then vanished. He waited for relief to flood through him, like it did whenever his mom snapped at his sisters to stop bullying him.

But relief didn't come. Instead, he felt a tug toward Mia, just like he'd felt when he'd had to leave his den behind.

He gazed back through the marsh. What if his mom had finally chased Mr. Scratch away and was sniffing for Uly at the forest's edge? Then again, what if he hopped back alone and was eaten by a rock or dissolved by a flower?

"Mia?" he called into the swamp.

Wincing, he gave his forepaw a great pull, and it came free.

"Mia, wait! I'm sorry!"

He splashed after her, sniffing. But Mia's unripe-apple scent was already lost among the mossy grays and strangled greens.

The swamp grew darker —— *stranger* than before. The trees stretched to great, tangled heights, their twisted branches nearly touching the sky before plummeting toward an algae moon that rippled on black waters.

Uly stopped to catch his breath. Mist coiled around his paws.

"Mia?" he whispered.

His voice was lost beneath the chanting of frogs.

El-dirtch.

El-dirtch.

El-dirtch.

In his darkest moments, Uly feared he'd never left the crack. That everything that had come since — the forest, the furless terror, this swamp — were all part of the same nightmare. He was afraid that his life in the Boulder Fields had been nothing more than a dream he would never have again.

"Mia!" he called, slightly louder.

There came a ruffling from above. He looked up and found a bone-white bird perched on the mossy limb of a cypress tree. Black stripes banded the bird's eyes. Spiny feathers jutted out the back of its head. Its neck was as coiled as a snake.

"Um, excuse me?" Uly whispered.

He wasn't sure if a bird of the swamp would be able to understand a fox of the stones, but he was willing to try.

"Ms. Bird?" Uly whispered again.

The bird's neck uncoiled, and she tilted a yellow eye down at him.

"Did you see a fox come this way? A fox like … me?"

The bird stared. Then it slowly recoiled its neck and pointed its bill toward a hole in the canopy. There, a solitary star glowed strange and red in the sky.

"She went … that way?" he asked.

The bird just stared and pointed. The star flickered.

"Okay," Uly whispered. "Um, thank you."

He followed the star, and the way grew easier. The ground was slimy but solid, and protected by a tunnel of cattails. The star provided the only light, bathing the tunnel in a bloody hue. Uly hadn't hopped far when he saw a tail bobbing ahead.

"Mia!" he called, relief tingling through him. "I'm sorry about what I said. My sisters told me about the yellow. And they lied *all the time*. So yeah, um, sorry."

The tail continued to move through the darkness.

"I'm sure your siblings are fine," he said, trying to catch up. "They probably just — hey, will you slow down a second?"

The tail exited the cattail tunnel and came to a halt.

As Uly drew closer, the tail dulled gray, developing stripes in the strange starlight.

"M-Mia?"

He froze. This was not Mia's tail. Not Mia's tail at all. Before he could even hiccup, the tail's owner whirled, reared up on its hind paws, and screamed.

THREE

Uly tried to scamper backward, but he tripped over his tail and fell hard. *"Oof!"*

The creature stopped screaming. It sat back on its hind legs, oily eyes staring through black markings. Its small, grotesque paws clutched a soft oval egg to its chest. Green yolk dripped from its teeth.

"Sorry. *Hic!* Sorry. *Hic!* I'm sorry," Uly said, trying to catch his shuddering breath. "I — I thought you were a — *hic* — friend of mine. *Sorry.*"

The raccoon slurped the yolk. And then it grinned.

Uly's heart beat faster. Did raccoons eat foxes? His sisters didn't have any scary stories about them.

The raccoon hunched over and sniffed a circle around him. It stuck its wet nose into his right ear and huffed. It did the

224

same to the other. Completing the circle, it stared at Uly and snickered.

"Heh heh," Uly said, not sure what they were laughing about.

The raccoon's strange paws held out the egg in offering.

"Oh, um" — Uly hopped closer — "thank you."

The egg popped between his teeth and slipped down his throat. It was salty and delicious and filled him with a touch of confidence.

"Do you know a way out of this place?" he asked the raccoon.

It nodded eagerly.

Uly's whiskers perked. "Will you show me?"

The raccoon grinned, rubbing together its tiny paws.

"Okay, um, great," Uly said. "Thank you. Um, a-after you."

He followed the striped tail, hopping over puddles and wriggling under roots, as the leaves shimmered and the shadows darkened under the light of the red star. They arrived at a slog of still black water.

Uly thought they'd hit a dead end, but then the raccoon padded across a floating log.

"Oh, um …," Uly said. "Okay. Yeah. Sure. I can do that."

He hopped onto the log, causing it to roll beneath his paws. He scrambled sideways, but the log only rolled the other way, thumping him onto his hip and flipping him over. The log started to sink, and Uly just managed to bound to its end and hop to solid ground before the swamp swallowed the log with a gurgle.

"Whew!" he said, trying to laugh.

When he turned around, the raccoon was gone.

"Um, h-hello?"

Uly found himself stranded in the middle of a pool, standing on a hump of mud barely big enough for his three paws. Squinting, he spotted the striped tail on a distant bank. The raccoon met his eyes and grinned. Then it slipped behind a trunk and did not appear on the other side.

"O … kay," Uly said.

He leaned out from the muddy island and peered into the water, trying to see how deep it went. Skeeters skated across his reflection, sending ripples across the red star and the patches of moonlight peeking through the canopy. He couldn't see a bottom. He was about to test the water's depth when a spider scrabbled across the surface, one tail from his island.

"Hic! Hic! Hic!" Uly hopped back, lifting each paw in turn.

The spider was as big as his *head*. He was certain it was about to leap onto his throat and drink his insides, but it continued to the far bank.

Uly waited for his hiccups to settle. The darkness dripped and swayed.

"Hello?" he whispered. "Rac— *hic* —coon? Are you com— *hic* —ing back?"

As if in response, the red star flashed, briefly flooding the swamp with light. Uly's eyes snapped upward. What he had thought were patches of moonlight were more of those strange white birds. Each sat on a nest balanced on a mossy branch, drooping low over the water.

The star flashed again, and the birds craned back their necks and began to *grawk* in unison, their voices echoing across the pool. Uly winced. This sounded nothing like the songs he'd heard in the Boulder Fields. It was dark and choked and made no sense.

The birds continued to *grawk* ... until something responded.

A smell boiled from the pool's black depths. Bubbles burst on the surface, releasing an ancient scent of mold and rot and long-dead things.

Uly went as still as a stick bug.

The birds pointed their bills toward the pool, eyes wide, necks uncoiling. The water began to stir. A *splash* here. A *slosh* here. Uly's whiskers stood alert as he tried to sense where the thing was. But it seemed to be ... everywhere.

Bigger than boulders.

Bigger than mountains.

A thousand mouths, each hungrier than the last ...

He gulped.

Waves continued to swirl around the pool until eventually coming together beneath the lowest branch, where a lone bird perched. The bird panted, eyes flashing toward the sloshing water but refusing to leave her nest behind.

Uly had a bad feeling about this. He tried to shut his eyes, but they were stuck open.

The other birds continued to caw. The frogs joined in, swelling their throats. And then the water exploded in an upward rush of roaring white. There was a *snap* and a *crunch* and a bone-chilling *grawk* as a toothy mouth dragged the bird underwater.

The other birds cawed toward the red star as the waves sloshed with bloody feathers. Several raccoons padded onto the shore and dug through the muck. They plucked the soft oval eggs buried there before fading back into the shadows.

Uly tried calling out to them, but his voice came out in a rasp. *"Help."*

The water stirred again.

FOUR

Uly cowered on his mud island.

"Um — *hic!* — excuse me?" he whispered to the nearest bird.

The bird uncoiled her neck and looked at him with one wide yellow eye. Her other eye was missing.

"Um — *hic* — hi," he said. "I'm — *hic* — not supposed to be here? I'm not a raccoon or a bird or — *hic* — an *egg*. So if you could — *hic* — please point your beak toward the way across this pool, then — *hic* — I'll just —"

The bird gave her bill a sharp *snip*, cutting him off. The other birds heard the sound and turned their bills toward Uly's island, red starlight gleaming in their eyes.

"Oh, um — *hic* — never mind," he said. "I can find my — *hic* — own way out."

Again, the birds craned back their necks and cawed. The water around Uly's island began to churn. There came a swish of scales to his left. A slosh of claws to his right. A wave curled with gleaming teeth. He hopped in circles, trying to keep the thing in front of him. But it was impossible.

He looked at the bird with pleading eyes. "I — I — I can't be eaten today! *Hic!* My mom is looking for me! And I never — *hic!* — apologized to my friend! And —"

Water splashed over his paws, silencing him. Uly dropped to his stomach and wrapped his tail around himself. He squeezed his eyes shut, willing his ears to look like leaves, his fur to look like moss.

The birds continued to caw. The pool continued to slosh. Any moment, the water would explode, and his body would be dragged under, ripped to pieces by the Golgathursh's countless mouths, digested in its swamp-sized —

"How the *squip* did you get all the way over there?"

Uly's eyes leapt open. There, on a bank just ten tails away, was Mia. He blinked a few times to make sure she wasn't just starlight shining on moss.

She rolled her eyes. "Don't look happy to see me or anything." She splashed along the shallows, trying to find a way to his island. "Lucky for you, I don't leave foxes behind anymore. Even if they do say mean things about my siblings."

The creature beneath the water sensed the splashing and swept toward the shore. Uly shook his head at Mia, trying to signal her to be quiet.

"I went back to the marsh to find you," she called, still splashing, "but you were gone. I thought the swamp had swallowed you!"

"Mia!" he hissed. "Get back! Get away from the shore!"

She didn't hear him. "But *then* I caught your scent and followed you here. Anyone ever tell you that you kinda smell like flower buds?"

The sloshing waves fell still near Mia. The thing in the water bubbled, waiting to strike. Uly couldn't watch her get eaten. He had to save her. But how?

Just then, another spider went scrabbling past his island. Without thinking, Uly seized its spiny leg and hurled it toward the bank. The spider landed with a frantic splash … but the Golgathursh didn't eat it. As if the spider were a pathetic offering.

The one-eyed bird above Uly threw back its bill and let out an awful choking laugh. The water swirled beneath it and then exploded in a roar of teeth. There was another *crack* and a *grawk* as the bird was dragged into the shallows.

Mia's ears shot up. Her eyes went wide.

"What was that?" she whispered, backing away from the shore.

Uly spoke through his teeth. *"What do you think?"*

Her whiskers went spiky. She believed him.

"Quick!" she said, searching the bank. "We have to find something to drag you over here!"

Uly was shocked. If he'd been in Mia's position, he would have fled the second the water exploded and never looked back. Just having her stick around filled his whiskers with confidence.

Mia gave up her search. "Looks like you're gonna have to swim to me."

234

Uly's confidence evaporated. *"What."*

"You're gonna have to *swim*," she said.

"What?"

Mia wrinkled her muzzle. "Did you really not hear me, or are you just pretending so you don't have to do it?"

His muzzle clamped shut.

"That's what I thought," she said.

Behind Uly, toothy mouths played tug-of-war with the bird's body, pulling it to pieces.

"Better hurry while it finishes chewing," Mia said.

Uly hopped up and down on his forepaw. "I never swam before!"

"It's easy!" she said. "It's like running. Just don't stop moving your paws."

"I never really ran before either!"

"Welp," she said, "maybe it's time you try."

Uly whimpered. It was the crack in the Boulder Fields all over again. Someone was forcing him to do something he knew in his paws he could not do. He bounced in a circle, searching for another way. He hated his withered paw that couldn't run or jump or swim. He hated his cowardice.

"You're not a baby anymore, Uly," Mia said. "I can't come grab you by the scruff and carry you over here." She fixed her eyes on his. "And if you don't at least try to swim, you're gonna make me break my promise not to leave any more foxes behind."

Uly stifled a whimper. Mia's tone made her sound cruel, like his sisters. But the words she used felt comforting, like something his mom would say. It put his whiskers in a tangle.

"Besides," Mia said in a chipper voice, "the water's only about a foot deep. Your paws can touch the bottom!"

He scowled at her. "I don't believe you."

"I know," she said. "Pretend like you do."

Behind him, the toothy mouths had slowed their chewing. The bird was nearly eaten.

Uly stared at the water, eyebrows shaking. "What do I do again?"

"Just jump in and —" Mia rolled onto her back and stuck her four paws in the air. Then, catching herself, she curled one paw to her chest and pedaled with three. "And just do *this* as hard as you can."

"Okay," he said, sliding his forepaw into the water. "Okay. Okay. Okay." With each *okay*, he made another hop forward — water rising to his chest, then to his chin. "Oka—"

The ground ended, and he was underwater. His breath bubbled. Murk clouded his eyes. He hiccupped, and water shot up his nostrils.

He started to panic but then remembered Mia's three legs pedaling the air. He tried it. At first, he swam forward instead of up, and his lungs strained. But then he kicked harder with his hind legs, and he rose stroke by stroke until his muzzle broke through the surface.

Uly gasped, coughing and spluttering as he continued to paddle.

"You've got it!" Mia said, voice shaking with relief. "See? Swimming is easy!"

His hind paw grazed something scaly.

"Augh. Hic! Augh! Hic! Augh!" he screamed. "It — *hic!* — touched me!"

"Don't worry," Mia said casually. "I hear the Gurblethrust is allergic to foxes."

"Ha ha — *hic!* — *grrblub!*" Uly laughed and hiccupped, and his muzzle went underwater.

He pedaled upward, again breaking through the surface.

Something slippery licked against his chest.

"Oh no, oh no, oh — hic! — no," he said.

"Psh," Mia said. "That's just Mortimer. He's a tickler."

"Ha ha — *ulp*. Don't make me laugh."

"Sorry! I'm trying to help!"

He was halfway to her now. Just five tails to go. His lungs stung with inhaled water. His legs were numb. He focused on Mia's smiling face and kept paddling.

Her eyes went wide with fear when she saw something behind him. "You have to swim faster, Uly."

"What is it?" he said, turning his head.

"Don't look!" she cried. "Just focus on me."

He locked his eyes on the blue swirl of hers, trying not to sink, trying not to think about the water opening behind him, sharp with teeth.

"The faster you get here, the faster I can clean you!" Mia said, voice shaking, trying to smile. "Ha ha! You're all covered in slime!"

Uly kicked his paws, but he didn't seem to be getting any closer to her. He felt like he was running in place.

"That's it!" she cried. "You're almost here! Just a few more tails ..."

Uly paddled as hard as he could. Mia seemed so happy to have him around. Even though no one had told her she had to. And that gave Uly enough strength to swim ten lakes.

Mia's jaw started to tremble. "Uly!" she screamed. "Watch ou—"

Uly felt a tug, and the world vanished in a splash. Water filled his senses.

"Ulyyyyyyyyy!"

Mia's silhouette grew faint and watery above as the Golgathursh dragged him into the pool's black depths.

FIVE

Uly screamed bubbles.

He tried paddling toward the surface, but the teeth clenched tighter around his paw. He tried clawing at the mouth that held him, but its scales were as solid as stone. The more he scrambled and scratched, the faster his breath streamed from his nostrils. Soon his air was spent.

The jaws of the Golgathursh dragged him deeper.

Funny. He couldn't even feel its teeth.

Here Uly was, about to die again. He could almost hear his sisters' mocking voices bubbling from the depths.

We won't have to clean you much longer, you know.

The Shrouded Fox will come for you.

The centipedes'll twine through your nostrils.

And that will be the end of Ewwwly.

Uly stopped struggling. His paws slowed. His lungs hitched. The water embraced him, and a warmth coursed through his body. Soon, the many toothy mouths would chew him up until he was nothing but bones. And maybe that was okay. Bones never had to worry about hunting. Or sisters. If Uly was nothing but bones, Mr. Scratch couldn't tell his mom to hurt him again.

Uly was surprised he'd survived as long as he did. He remembered the king snake flashing from the crack, sinking its fangs into Ava's haunch. It should have been him who'd been bitten that day. Then his mom wouldn't have had to choose between him and his sisters.

He stared up, up, up, toward the pool's distant surface. At least he'd spent his last few days with a friend. Or someone who acted like one, at least …

His heart sank when he realized he'd never warned Mia to stay away from cracks. He'd been too afraid to tell her his story, worried she'd think he was worthless, and now the kit who'd cleaned him and fed him and even come back for him after he'd been mean didn't know about the snakes that lurked in dark places.

He had to get back and warn her.

Uly struggled against the teeth that held his paw, jerking to break free. But he was no match for the stony jaws of the Golgathursh, which dragged him deeper and deeper into the crystalline darkness.

He was about to give up forever when a light flashed from above. The red star beamed through the murky water ... and Uly saw the Golgathursh. The whole thing. It filled the pool — a whirlwind of scaly limbs circling up through the water.

He saw the monster for what it really was. Not one creature with many mouths and limbs, but many creatures that looked like giant lizards. And Uly realized his sisters had lied to him.

He looked down at the thing that held his paw. It was more than just a crooked grin. He saw its giant eye — mottled and yellow with a sharpened pupil — and he kicked at it. The eye was soft and flinched at the sharpness of his claws. Its teeth clenched tighter, and he kicked again.

The jaws rolled, and Uly flipped through the water, turning and tumbling. The night sky whirled beneath him, and the pool's bottom spun overhead, blurring together. Uly swallowed more water. He thought he might throw up. He thought he might pass out. He thought he might drown if he swallowed one more drop ...

But there came a *snap*, and he was free. With his hind paws, he pushed up off the scaly snout that had held him and swam up through the great whirlwind of limbs and mouths and eyes. He paddled toward the red star, kicking off the giant lizards' many spiny limbs, keeping away from their toothy ends, as he propelled himself upward.

A couple of tails from the surface, a mouth opened beneath him. Uly made himself flat, spreading his paws wide, barely catching either end of the snout that struck his belly as it roared out of the water and launched him into the air.

He landed on the bank with a *splat* and scrambled across the muck as the great mouth rattled and then sank back into the pool, empty.

Six

Uly found Mia hiding among the leaves, staring back toward the pool.

She whimpered and pawstepped, waiting to see if he would resurface. It was such a nice sight that he decided to sit and watch for a minute while his heart pumped some feeling back into his limbs.

Mia, still watching the water, drew in a breath and held it. When the air burst out of her, she drew in another. It burst out, and she did it again.

"You're gonna make yourself light-headed," Uly said.

Mia jumped. Her nose jerked toward him, and a smile burst across her face. "Uly!"

She romped over to nip and lick at his ears. He didn't mind it so much this time.

"You're not drowned!" she said. "You're not eaten! You're — you're — you're *okay!*"

244

"Yeah," Uly said. "I guess I am."

She squinted as he shook himself dry, showering her in droplets.

"Holy *squip*," she said when he was finished. "How'd you make it out in one piece?"

"Oh, um" — he looked at his chest — "I didn't."

Mia's jaw fell open. "It got your *paw*!"

It was true. Uly's withered foreleg was gone. Taken.

She gave the remaining stump a sniff. "It snipped clean off! There's no blood or anything!"

"Maybe that's why it never worked so good," he said. "Not enough blood." He sighed. "At least now I don't have to carry it around anymore."

"Ha! That's the first joke I've heard you make!" She shook her muzzle in disbelief. "You don't seem scared or anything."

The feeling was still tingling back into Uly's limbs. "I … don't know what I am."

He remembered that he hadn't apologized to Mia yet. Only to a raccoon's butt.

"I'm sorry, Mia," he said. "Sorry for saying that stuff about your brothers and sister. Whenever my sisters told me stories — even true ones — they always did it to hurt me. And I ... I don't want to be like them." He looked into her eyes. "I don't know what happened to your siblings. Really."

Mia's mouth twitched. "How about let's talk about it later and get out of this place?"

Uly gave her a lopsided smile. "Sounds good."

They continued north, side by side, away from the red star.

"So what *was* that thing?" she asked. "Was it really the Gurg— Grog— Gorg—"

"Yep."

"And all those limbs were part of the same —"

"Uh-huh."

"And it had a thousand —"

"More than that maybe."

"Wow," Mia said.

He decided not to tell her what he'd realized in the belly of the swamp — that the Golgathursh was nothing but a bunch of big lizards and that all he'd had to do was scratch one of their eyes to escape. That didn't sound nearly as scary as it had been.

He leapt over a stone and remembered something important. "Oh, um … don't jump over any cracks, okay?"

"Huh?" she said.

"Just, if you see a crack, let me jump over it first. I'll let you know if it's safe."

Mia giggled. "You got it, weirdo."

They continued out of the swamp and back into the forest, steering clear of even the smallest of puddles.

A SHRIEK CUT through the Antler Wood.

The little one's heart leapt, and her paws almost followed. But then the shriek ended in a snort, and she realized her sister had only been laughing.

"Lizards?" the third kit said, still giggling. "Everyone knows there are no lizards that big! This story is so dumb."

"Uhhh," the beta said. "We've got some bad news for you, Iffy."

"There *are* lizards that big," the alpha said. "They're called alligators."

"What?" the third kit said and scoffed. "Nooooo."

She looked at the little one, who slowly nodded.

"But ... ," the third kit said. "But I've *eaten* lizards. And if there are ones out there as big as logs, with mouths as long as *me*, then ..."

She gulped. Her ears folded, and her whiskers sank as she slunk back toward the den.

Three little foxes.

The eyes in the cavern gleamed with moonlight. "Mia and Uly had found their way out of the swamp. They continued north until they were clear of the forest. But the kits were not safe. Not by a season."

The little one curled her tail around herself. She hadn't thought they were.

"In fact," the storyteller continued, "the fox kits might have remained in the forest if they knew what horrors awaited them on the other side …"

THE LILAC
KINGDOM

ONE

The moment the trees cleared, Mia took off across bronze hills, leaves trailing in her wake. The ground moved swiftly beneath her paws. The weeds that would have tripped her up a few weeks ago now only brushed her underbelly. Stones were cleared in a single leap. Mia had seen her mom bound across the Eavey Wood as if feathers sprouted from her paws. Now that freedom was Mia's.

She sprinted to the top of a grassy hill, lifted a paw, and sniffed. She ran to the top of another and sniffed again. Her nose searched the grasses for her mom's apple-scented fur. But all she could smell was the tart scent of blushing leaves. Chill breezes loosed them from the branches, whirling and tumbling them into great rustling piles of yellow and orange.

Autumn was even more beautiful than she'd hoped. It filled Mia's senses with more smells and colors than she'd dreamed possible. But her heart couldn't quite feel it. There was a bite in the air. The sun no longer warmed her fur. Her Golden-Eyed Day was only weeks away — the day she would have left the Eavey Wood to start a life of her own.

She wasn't ready.

Mia checked the mouth of the forest, where Uly was just now hopping out. He'd shed his second coat, and his fur was growing bright red. She turned her nose northward and sniffed one last time. The air was itchy with leaf dust. But it was foxless.

She returned to the forest's edge.

"What's your mom smell like?" Uly asked, nibbling a burr from one of his hind paws.

"Like me, I guess," Mia said.

Uly sniffed the breeze while she stifled a whimper.

Her mom had told her to travel to the far side of the forest. But her mom wasn't there. Had she been captured by another trap? Mia swallowed. Had she gone to the baby-bush to find a new kit? She shook the thought away, reminding herself that baby-bushes weren't real.

Mia scanned the hills stretching to the horizon, wondering where to search next.

"Where's your home?" she asked Uly.

"Oh, um — a ... *achoo!*"

He sneezed but didn't answer. Not for the first time, Mia suspected that he hadn't told her everything about how he'd come to be lost in the forest. Then again, she hadn't told him that her mom thought she was dead. She couldn't get her mouth to say the words.

She turned her attention to the horizon. Her mom had told her to find a den just like the one they'd had in the Eavey Wood. With sandy loam and a sipping creek and good cover for the entrance. If Mia could find a place that had all of those things, she might find her mom.

She sniffed until her nose caught a drying channel tucked between the hills. "Let's go through there. It'll keep us hidden from predators while we head north."

Uly sniffed too. "Oh. Oh yeah. That's the way I need to go anyway."

The channel led them to a rocky scramble. Mia leapt up easily, pausing every so often to check on Uly, who was having trouble keeping his balance on the teetering rocks.

"You got this!" she called to him.

He nodded, panting, and made another small hop.

After a long, difficult climb, the sky reddened with dusk, and they arrived at the craggy shadow of a cliff that blocked their way northward.

"Welp," Mia said, sniffing up and up, "*that's* inconvenient."

Uly hopped next to her, out of breath. "It's a cliff."

"Y'know," she said as kindly as she could. "I think you might be right. Wait here."

She bounded up a slope that rose steeply to the east and sniffed the wide expanse of rolling hills. There were two ways they could go. Northwest, along a rocky path that curved around the base of the cliffs. Or east, down a clear trail that wove between the hills.

The way east looked more manageable for Uly's foreleg. But when Mia

256

sniffed the hills, she caught a scent that made her eyes water. Gray wisps curled against the horizon, choking the sky with ash. Mia squinted through the haze and found great sections of hill cut with black pathways.

Roads.

She bounded back to the channel.

"This way," she said as she passed Uly, following the cliff face west. "Fast."

"What is it?" Uly said. "What'd you see?"

"Humans."

He followed without any more questions.

Clouds swept overhead, extinguishing the sunset.

"We should find somewhere to sleep," Uly said.

Mia nodded. Over the past few weeks, they'd become experts at finding safe hovels in the forest. But this land was open and had few places to hide. The most promising spots were thick with animal scent.

As the sky faded from gray to rumbling black, they continued along the cliff's base as it gradually shrank into the ground, opening onto a scraggly hill. At the top of the hill, great violet clouds billowed, silhouetting black stones that towered toward the sky.

"Pretty," Mia said, her whiskers electric.

The clouds flashed lightning teeth, and the sky cracked so loudly it seemed it might split in two.

Uly's ears folded. *"That's* pretty to you?"

"Yeah! In a spooky sorta way." Mia bounded up the hill as raindrops started to fall. "Come on! We can hide in that rock pile until the rain passes."

Uly hesitated. "I ... can't really *do* hills."

"Sure you can!" she called back. "It's just like the swamp. One paw at a time."

Uly made a determined face and followed, climbing the hill in zigzags. Mia bounded up a few foxtails and then turned to watch her friend.

"Almost there!" she sang brightly through the drizzle.

Uly stopped to pant. "Are you kidding? We're not even close!"

"True ... But we're almost there to *partway* there!"

Mia ignored Uly's grumbling and gazed through the rain, beyond the hilltop to where the black stones speared the sky. She sniffed, hoping for a whiff of apple. But instead she caught a smooth, intoxicating scent. She breathed deep, letting it stir her whiskers and make her fur stand on end. The sky rippled with thunder.

"Do you smell that?" Mia called down the hill. "It's like —"

"Don't say peaches and centipedes," Uly said, taking another miserable hop. "It didn't work the first time, and it's not gonna —"

"No, really!" *Snff snff.* "It's like flowers! Like" — *snfffff* — "*lilac!*"

Uly stopped climbing. He turned back and began his slow zigzags down the hill.

"Wait!" Mia cried. "Where are you going?"

He kept descending.

"Uly, stop!"

He looked over his shoulder, eyebrows trembling. "That's Mr. Scratch's scent."

Mia perked her ears. She wasn't sure she'd heard him right through the rain.

"Who the squip is Mr. *Scratch*?"

"He's ...," Uly said. "He's my dad."

Mia quirked her head. "That's a *good* thing, right?"

Uly shook his head.

Mia's own father was a hazy memory — a musty scent that brought fresh kills to her and her siblings every morning when they were babies.

She sniffed toward the top of the hill again, catching the lilac.

Foxes mark the borders of their kingdoms using their family's scent, Miss Vix had told her and her siblings. *The smell is meant as a warning for other foxes: Keep away, or else ...*

Mia also remembered what her teacher had said about staying away from strangers. But it was different when they were related to you, wasn't it? What dad would try to kill his own kit? No dad. That was who.

"Uly, we *have* to go this way," she called through the rain. "My mom wouldn't have gone anywhere near the humans and their roads."

The sky shuddered. The rain grew heavier. Uly couldn't stop shaking.

Mia furrowed her brow. She could understand being afraid of a Golgathursh. But not of a *dad*. She wanted to grab Uly by the scruff and drag him up the hill. But that hadn't gone over very well in the swamp. She needed a different approach.

She descended until she was just uphill of him. "Your dad might have food for us. You love food."

Uly's muzzle trembled. "You don't know him."

Mia started to walk. "What did he do that was so bad?"

He hopped alongside her, searching the ground, as if debating something. "He … he bit my sister."

"Ah, that's no big deal," Mia said, angling her paws ever so slightly uphill. "I bit my siblings all the time."

Uly stopped. "It — it was worse than that. I don't know. I'm not as good at telling scary stories as my sisters."

"You mean to tell me," Mia said, spinning around and continuing to climb backward, "you're more afraid of your dad than you are a Gurglethork?"

Uly scowled and hopped to catch up. *"Golgathursh."*

"That's what I said. Geekathirst. That thing was *way* scarier. But we made it through together, right?" She flipped around and continued at a trot. "We'll be reeeaaaal sneaky. Your dad can't catch both of us. Besides, look! You're almost to the top."

Uly scowled when he realized she had led him in a diagonal up the hill. He flipped around and started hopping back down.

A snarl rose in Mia's throat. *"Humans* are that way!"

He stopped and hung his head.

"You think your *dad* is bad?" she snapped. "Miss Potter broke my mom's *paw*. She boiled off a fox's skin, then replaced his eyes with shiny rocks and stuffed him full of *grass*. That's what humans do."

Uly shivered, rain dampening his coat. Thunder rumbled overhead.

"Uly," Mia said softly. "Please. I can't go back to the cage again."

He met her eyes. "And I can't face my dad again."

They stared at each other. Raindrops dripped from their noses.

Mia's heart made a tumble. "So I guess this is goodbye, then?"

Lightning clawed the sky, and Uly saw something behind her. His expression changed from shame to horror. Mia turned around.

At first, all she could make out was a skull floating in the darkness. But then the shadows of its sockets crinkled.

"Its sweat will only serve as spice," the skull grumbled.

Lightning flashed again, illuminating the creature's eyes, the slick black hair of its paws, its back a mound of fur and muscle. *Badger.* Mia had only ever seen one from a distance, when Miss Vix had chased it away from the den. Its jaws could pop a kit's skull as easily as a gooseberry.

The badger sucked rain through its gray teeth. "Yes, a long climb it's made, but its sweat will only spice its meat."

TWO

The badger lunged and head-butted Uly, who went tumbling down the hill and flopped unconscious at the bottom. The badger muscled after him, but Mia clamped her teeth onto its stubby tail. Her mouth filled with slimy foulness, but she yanked back with all her might.

The badger roared and rounded, chomping into her throat. The pain was bigger than any Mia had ever felt. She tried to yelp, but the badger's jaws squeezed tighter, and Mia's breath stopped short.

She kicked with her back paws and caught the badger's eye. Its jaws released. She tried to scamper away, but its fangs caught her by the tail. She heard the rip before she felt the sting. Her tail went cold.

Mia slipped along the hill's edge while the badger hurled itself after her, teeth grinding. The smell of her own blood made

Mia light-headed, and the hill threatened to upturn beneath her paws. She shook the spots from her eyes and kept running.

There was nowhere to hide on this hill. No mole burrows. No brambles. But now that Mia's legs were a little longer, she could reach high spots a badger's stubby legs could not.

She wove sidelong through the scraggly branches until she could no longer feel its gray breath on her heels. She bounded over the lip of the hill, darted toward the tallest rock she could find, and leapt on top of it. She whirled and watched for the skull to come huffing over the hill's edge.

Her tail throbbed. Her heart could barely keep up with her breath.

The badger wasn't coming.

Uly.

Mia leapt off the rock and sprinted back to the hill's edge. The badger was barreling toward her friend, who lay at the hill's base, eyes closed, forepaw twitching.

She would never reach him in time.

"Uly!" she cried through the lashing rain. "Uly, *wake up*!"

He didn't stir. The badger went after him like a mudslide.

Mia ran along the hill's crest until she was right over them. She leapt. The hill fell away beneath her paws as she soared down, rain hissing past her ears. She struck the mud and then rolled, whipping through branches. On her final roll, she managed to get her paws underneath her and then bounded toward her friend.

She realized she had never wanted anything more than for Uly to survive. She realized this as the badger seized him by the throat and shook his body like a loose rabbit skin.

With one last leap, Mia caught the badger by the ear and ripped as hard as she could. The badger roared in pain, dropping Uly's body. It thrashed blindly in every direction while Mia backed away.

When the badger regained its senses, it fixed its black eyes on her, licking Uly's blood from its gray teeth. Mia snarled and began to circle the creature, remembering her fighting lessons. *Stand with your side facing the enemy. Keep your legs stiff and your hackles sharp. Try to get behind them.*

266

The badger lashed, and its fang caught Mia's forehead. She stifled a cry but continued to circle. The badger attacked again, and Mia just managed to lift her paw in time to feel one of her claws ripped out. She screamed and limped away, wanting to put as much space between her and the badger as she could. But then she saw Uly lying in the mud, and she hesitated.

"I wonder what it last ate," the badger grumbled, licking its lips. "Hopefully not a shrew. I do hate shrews."

Blood trickled into Mia's eyes. The badger was going to tear her apart, piece by piece.

Thunder tore through the air and then faded ... into a growl. Mia turned to find a shadow at the top of the hill. It leapt over her, and the badger recoiled, snarling and spitting at its new opponent.

The badger distracted, Mia limped to the bottom of the hill. She found Uly under one of the scraggly branches. His tongue hung, bloody, out of his mouth.

"*Uly!* Uly, *please* talk to me."

She licked the blood from his muzzle, and his eyes made the smallest of cracks. He hefted his head and sniffed at the badger's gray drool on his coat. "Ugh. What stinks?"

Mia laughed and then sobbed in relief.

Uly's muzzle clamped shut as he gazed beyond her toward the top of the hill. She followed his eyes. The fight was lit by lightning flashes. Jaws crunched ears. Claws sliced clouds of fur. Black droplets spattered the mud.

It was a fox. A fox had saved their lives.

"Should we help him?" Mia asked.

When Uly didn't answer, she turned and found him gone. She sniffed through the rain, following his flower-bud scent around the side of the hill.

She smelled the cave before she saw it. Deep and cold and wet.

"Uly?" Mia called into the darkness. "Uly, what are you doing? We have to help him. If all three of us just —"

"No," Uly said. His whispers echoed. "He'll — *hic* — kill me."

Mia squinted into the cave. "Why would he kill you? He just saved our lives!"

"He saved — *hic!* — *your* life."

"You're being silly," she said. "There are already enough scary things in the world without adding other foxes to the list. Especially ones in your own family."

"Not other foxes," Uly said. "Mr. Scratch."

A roar echoed from the top of the hill. Mia peered around the cave's overhang. The fight was almost won. The fox struck at the badger, driving it down the hill.

"It's blood and parts!" the badger spat. "Meat and fur and nothing else!"

The fox stood strong until the badger faded into the graying rain, west toward where the humans dwelled. Once it was gone, the fox collapsed to his side. Mia took a step toward him.

"Mia," Uly whispered from the cave. "Don't. Please."

"He's just a fox, Uly," she said, and hobbled up the hill.

The rain slowed to a drizzle. The fox lay still. His chest rose and fell, huffing fog. Blood ran down his coat. He seemed so helpless, like he couldn't hurt a mouse.

Mia took a step closer, and the fox rolled onto his stomach, wincing. "Ah. There you are," he said. "I thought you'd fled."

She took a step back. The fur on his face was so black it made his amber eyes glow like a sunset. His muzzle was long and powerful, and moon-bright fangs stood sharp outside his mouth.

She swallowed. "How'd you beat that badger?"

The fox began to clean his wounds. "I almost didn't. Were it not for your bravery, I wouldn't have been able to surprise him." He grinned at her. "If I didn't know better, I'd say you'd been fighting badgers since the day you were born."

270

Mia's whiskers twitched with embarrassment. "What, that? That was nothing."

The fox continued to clean his wound.

"What's your name?" she asked.

With another wince, the fox pushed upright and bowed his head. "My name is Wynn."

Mia smirked. So *not* Mr. Scratch. That must've been a name Uly came up with.

"And yours?" Wynn asked.

"Mia."

"It's a pleasure to meet you, Mia."

The air became laced with lilac, making her nose twitch. When she was a kit, the thought of marking territory had made her gag. But now it confused her. If this scent was meant to keep other foxes out, why did it smell so … *pretty*?

Wynn took a step toward her, and she took a step away.

He smiled, his fangs white and gleaming. "I was only going to clean your wound. It seems that creature hurt your forehead. And your throat."

My claw and my tail too, she thought. But she didn't go any closer.

"You are welcome to remain here," Wynn said, gazing toward the towering rocks. "It's a dark night for a fox kit all alone."

Mia resisted the urge to look at the cave. If Uly would just come out of hiding, he'd realize there was nothing to be afraid of.

"I, uh, can't stay," she said, looking north beyond the rock pile toward a great chasm that broke the land. "I need to find my mom."

"Then you're in luck," Wynn said. "My scent draws vixens to these rocks. If your mother comes within a thousand foxtails of this place, rest assured she'll end up here."

"Oh," Mia said. "I didn't know that."

She sniffed the landscape. The marshes and the forest in the south. The smoky hills to the east. The chasm to the north that wrapped around to the cave in the west. Finding her mom felt as impossible as finding a whisker in a field.

Also, Mia was hurt. She had no idea how long it would be before she could hunt again.

Moonlight broke through the clouds, making the black stones of the tower shine.

"I'll stay," she said. "Just for tonight."

"Good," Wynn said. "You'll find a place to rest near the rocks' summit. The stones will divert the rain, and there are vixens to clean your wounds."

He turned to leave, then paused. His nose tilted toward the cave. *Snff snff.* His muzzle wrinkled only a moment. And then Wynn vanished into the evening.

Mia considered returning to the cave to wish Uly a good night but thought better of it.

"Let him pout," she said, and began her long climb to the rocks.

THREE

Mia sat on a high stone perch and watched another storm sweep over the Lilac Kingdom. Rain cascaded off the stones, stirring the mist in the chasm and slicking the scraggly hill into a muddy waterfall that flooded into the cave. She tried not to worry about Uly.

It had been three days since Mia had climbed the rock pile, and she still hadn't had a chance to visit her friend. Wynn was always watching from his roost that overlooked the vixens' quarters.

"Come away from the rain, child," a voice said behind her.

It was Odette, whose fur was as red as raspberries.

"You haven't finished your squirrel heart."

This was Mercy, whose fur was as red as elk's blood.

Mia slipped into the faint light of the rocky overhang and folded her paws around the heart. She took tiny bites, trying not to think about how hungry Uly must be down in that cave. It wasn't her fault if he wanted to cower in the wet darkness while she remained dry beneath the rocks.

"There," Odette said, eyes reflecting the storm. "Isn't that better?"

"Sure," Mia said, licking the blood from her beard.

Mercy lay quiet in the shadows. The vixens of the Lilac Kingdom had a strange, glazed look in their eyes. Mia tried not to look directly at them. They reminded her of Mr. Tod's eyes.

Still, the vixens were kind to her. Odette had cleaned her fur and soothed her wounds, and Mercy had shown her where the food was buried. Mia's claw and forehead were feeling better, but her tail and throat were slow to heal. She had spent the days napping and cleaning her wounds, and feasting on squirrels and serpents. But she was starting to feel restless.

"When does Wynn go hunting?" she asked once her squirrel heart was finished.

"*Whisper*, child," Mercy said, glancing up toward Wynn's roost.

"Our husband's senses are as sharp as starlight," Odette said.

"Oh," Mia said, lowering her voice, though she wasn't sure why. "Sorry."

"Why do you want to know?" Odette asked.

Mia wanted to check on Uly. He had to be cold and hungry and wondering where she was. But she didn't dare sneak down to the cave, in case Wynn saw her and asked where she was going. She had come to trust the lord of the Lilac Kingdom. He had provided her food and shelter and asked nothing in return. But if she led Wynn to Uly, Uly might never forgive her.

"I just wanted to hunt something," Mia said. "My tail's starting to feel better, and these squirrel hearts are too gushy."

"No need to worry your ears, child," Odette said.

"Name a thing," said Mercy, "and Wynn will hunt it for you."

"Once our stores are empty, of course," Odette said.

Mia looked at the pile of dead squirrels in the corner of their quarters. It would be days before they were eaten.

"Um," she said. "I also need to find my mom."

"Why, child?" Mercy asked. "The lilac scent will draw her here."

"Right," Mia said, looking away from the vixen's glazed eyes. "Right."

She didn't ask, *But what if it doesn't?*

"Settle, child," Odette said. "No need to rush. You don't realize you're in a good place."

"The best place," Mercy said.

Mia glanced through the cracks in the quarters, across the Lilac Kingdom. There was no sand. No sipping creek. No weedy cover. Only rocks and gushy hearts and endless storms.

"I ... like this place," Mia said, not wanting to sound ungrateful.

"No," Mercy said, "you don't."

"But you will," said Odette.

FOUR

That night, Mia waited for the vixens to fall asleep and then crept out of the quarters, as she had every night before. She watched the hill for a long time. Somewhere wolves howled. When the moon was high, a shadow slipped from Wynn's roost, stalked through the scraggly branches, and then vanished into the mists.

"Finally," Mia whispered.

She grabbed a squirrel haunch from the stores and trotted toward the caves, passing an upright stone.

"Good evening," the stone said.

Mia jolted and dropped the haunch. Moonlight shined on the black fur of Wynn's face. He perched on the rock above her, throwing a shadow, long and sharp.

She tried to laugh. "I thought you were a rock."

Wynn only stared at her, and Mia felt a chill. She could've sworn she'd seen his shadow padding down the hill. But it must have been a trick of the moonlight. Or the sleepy lilac scent.

"And where are you headed this night?" he asked.

"Oh, um, I thought I smelled my mom." She pawed at the squirrel haunch. "This is for her."

Wynn leapt from the rock onto the path between her and the cave. "I would advise you remain close to your quarters. The clouds are on the move tonight, and dark things go sniffing when the moon is obscured." He smiled his bright fangs. "If a vixen comes anywhere near this place, rest assured I will tell you."

"Oh," Mia said, trying to sound relieved. "Good." She started back toward the vixens' quarters, but then turned right back around again. "But I have to leave at some point. I can't just stay here forever, waiting for my mom to show up. That would be ... dumb."

"Of course." Wynn bowed his head. "And you're welcome to leave anytime you wish." The moon made an unnatural flicker in his eyes. "But the snows will fall soon, and all scents will be trapped beneath the ice."

"Oh," Mia said, watching mists coil in the chasm. "Right."

He stepped so close that she could smell the blood from his last kill. "I would have you remain here through the winter months, Mia. For your safety."

"Oh ... um, no thanks."

"Your first winter can be very difficult. Many don't survive."

"Good to know," she said.

Miss Vix had told her the same thing. Winter was the fiercest predator. But that was the least of Mia's worries right then. She still needed to bring Uly food and clean his wounds. She still needed to heal so they could continue north and find her mom.

"Your muzzle is whitening nicely," Wynn said. "Good coat. Strong teeth. You will make a fine vixen in the years to come." He smiled. "And one who can fight off badgers, as well."

Mia avoided his eyes. "Maybe ... but I still want to see my mom."

Wynn leapt back to his perch, scanning his kingdom. "I am unable to guarantee your safety if you stray from your quarters. Some of the rocks are unstable. A cave winds through the base of this hill. The ground could collapse beneath you."

Mia stared at her paws. This made her want to check on Uly all the more.

Wynn nodded toward the squirrel's haunch. "I would also advise you not to bring food out into the open. Dark things lurk in the mists at the edge of this kingdom. And in the cave. The smell could draw them out."

Mia stared at the squirrel haunch and thought, *Uly must be so hungry.* Then she picked it up and choked it down in a gulp.

Wynn continued to stare at her.

She cleared her throat. "Welp, back to the stones with me, I guess." She turned to leave, then paused. "Only ..."

"Yes?"

She remembered Mercy's and Odette's words and turned around. "I have this craving."

He bowed. "Name it. You are my guest."

She tried to think of something difficult to find.

"Peaches and centipedes," she said.

Wynn's eyes widened a little. Then he smiled. "I'll see what I can do."

"Thanks," Mia said. "You're the best."

Later that night, once Wynn's tail had slipped down the hill, Mia crept out of her quarters and along the northern chasm. Her paw accidentally nudged a pebble over the edge, and it whirled down, clacking once against the cliff's side before plunging into the mist. She shuddered and continued down the hill, into the cave.

"Uly?" she whispered, sloshing through paw-deep water.

A soft wind murmured through the darkness. There was a shuffling above, then a small splash.

"I'm here," he whispered.

"Hi!" Mia said. She couldn't stop her stinging tail from wagging. "How are you? I couldn't smell you! Are you okay?"

"Shh," Uly said.

His shining eyes slowly looked up. Mia followed them to the cave's ceiling. The shadows there shivered. Bats. Thousands of them. Folded in tiny bundles.

"Oh," she whispered, flattening her ears.

Bats were sharp, diseased things. If disturbed, they would pour down in a black avalanche, plunging their tiny fangs into her and Uly until they were bled dry.

She sloshed forward as quietly as she could. "How's your neck doing?"

"It's fine," he said.

When he didn't say more, she smirked. "I'm okay too, y'know. Thanks for asking."

"Right," he said. "Sorry."

Uly hopped into the faint light, making little splashes. There came another rustle from above, and the foxes cowered, eyes wide, waiting to see if the bats would awaken.

When the rustling fell still, Mia studied her friend. His fur was covered in mud. It was no wonder she couldn't smell him.

"No, *I'm* sorry," she said. "Sorry it took me so long to get down here. Wynn doesn't leave the rocks very often. And he won't let me take food out of the vixens' quarters."

"It's okay," Uly said. "I'm used to being hungry."

It was so pathetic Mia wasn't sure whether to whimper or laugh.

"You should come up to the rocks!" she whispered brightly. "There's lots of food and nice ladies that clean your face."

Uly shook his head. "If Mr. Scratch sees me, he'll kill me."

"Riiiiight," Mia said. "But what if he *doesn't*? What if your dad's not as bad as you think? He fed me and gave me a good place to sleep. He even said I could stay here through the winter if I wanted."

"Easy for you to say," Uly said. "You still have all your paws."

Mia huffed, irritated. "No one cares about that. And your dad's name is *Wynn*, by the way. Not *Mr. Scratch*."

Uly trembled. He hadn't really stopped trembling.

Mia gave up the argument. Uly was afraid of everything, and there was nothing she could do to talk him out of it.

A drip echoed somewhere deep in the darkness, swiveling her ears.

"How far back does it go?"

"I dunno," Uly said. "I haven't left this spot. Far, I think."

Another drip echoed deep in the cave's throat.

A breeze blew into the cave, and Mia thought she smelled lilac.

"I should get back before the vixens wake up," she said. She gave Uly's muzzle a lick. "But at least let me clean some of this mud —"

"Don't," he said, wrenching his head away. "He'll smell me."

Mia pulled back, a little hurt. *"Fine,"* she said. "We'll leave tomorrow. My throat's feeling better, and my claw's almost healed enough for walking. Not sure my tail will ever grow a white tip, though."

Uly stared into the water around his forepaw. "I … I don't want to leave."

Mia gave her head a shake. "Wait, *huh*?"

She spoke a little too loudly, and the ceiling shivered, making them both crouch.

Once the bats quieted, Uly's eyes shined toward the entrance. "My mom's up there. I can smell her."

Mia quirked her head. "You sure?"

"Yeah. I didn't think she'd come here so soon. My sisters must have left to start their dens. Either that or something happened to them."

Mia thought of the two vixens in the roost. Odette and Mercy. Their glazed eyes. Their strange manners. Could one of them really be Uly's mom?

"I hate to say it, Uly," Mia said, "but the vixens up there seem ... well, *happy*."

Just a weird *sort of happy,* she didn't say.

"They're not," Uly said.

Mia narrowed her eyes. "Are you sure you're not just being selfish?"

Uly stared at his forepaw.

"What's your mom's name? Odette? Mercy?"

"I don't know," he said. "I just called her Mom."

"Okay, what's she look like?"

"Um ... like me?"

Mia examined his muddy face. Little black wisps were forming on his muzzle, and his sunset eyes were blazing away the last of the blue. She almost told him he was starting to look more like his dad than anything but then thought better of it.

"Oh," Uly said. "I just remembered something. My mom has the top of one of her ears missing."

"Great!" Mia said. "I'll go see which vixen is missing part of an ear and then tell her you're here! We can all leave together!"

"But," Uly whispered, "what if *he* follows her down here, and he … *finds* me?"

"Well, Uly," Mia said, "either we leave or we stay. You can't have it both ways."

When he didn't answer, she sloshed toward the cave mouth. "I'll go find your mom and come for you next time Wynn goes hunting. We'll all sneak out of here. No problem."

Uly did not look encouraged there in the darkness.

"Come on," she said. "Have I ever led you astray? And remember, following that raccoon's tail in the swamp doesn't count. That was all you."

He sighed in defeat.

"Sleep tight!" she whispered. "Don't let the cave bats bite!"

■■■■

As the horizon grew hazy with dawn, Mia crept back to the vixens' quarters.

"And where have you been this night?"

Wynn stared down at her from his high roost.

"Good morning!" she said quickly. "Did you get that food I asked for?"

He nodded toward the ground at a shriveled apple filled with worms.

Mia wrinkled her muzzle. "Ew."

"You did not answer my question," Wynn said.

Mia looked toward the chasm to the north. "I was just trying to figure out where I wanted to search for my mom, now that I'm all healed up. I'll probably leave tonight or tomorrow."

Wynn narrowed his eyes.

"I know, I know," Mia said, rolling hers. "Dark things in the mists. Don't want to draw their attention and stuff."

"The creatures are not the only thing you should fear."

"What do you mean?"

He sniffed down the hill. "I believe I've smelled an intruder. A male fox. Young." Wynn's sunset eyes flashed toward her. "Have you smelled anything?"

"Nope," Mia said.

"Mm." A growl crackled in his throat.

"Just out of curiosity," she said, "what would you do if a fox *did* come here? Chase him off like you did the badger?"

"I would kill him," Wynn said.

"Oh," Mia said, gulping. "That's a relief."

She wanted to ask if that included his own son, but that would give Uly away.

Wynn leapt from his perch, landing so close Mia had to move her tail. "With all of these creatures sneaking into my kingdom — badgers, foxes — I am going to advise that you delay the search for your mother."

"But … if I wait too long, I might lose her."

"Perhaps," Wynn said. "Is that not what growing up is all about?"

A heat spread to Mia's ears. He didn't know that she'd had to leave her den too soon. That she never got to say goodbye.

"How come you want me to stay so bad?" she asked.

He chuckled. "It is you who wants to stay. You just don't realize it yet."

He padded circles around her, and Mia turned her paws, keeping him in sight.

"You have everything you could ever want here, Mia," Wynn said. "Food. Safety. Vixens to call sisters. If you desire anything else, all you have to do is name it."

"I *told* you like three times already," she said. "I want to find my mom."

He continued to pace. "This is the season you would have left your den, is it not?"

"Yeah. So?"

"Your eyes are nearly golden. You're now able to make choices for yourself."

"That's true," she said. "And I want to leave."

Wynn stopped pacing with a sigh. "Perhaps I was mistaken. It seems you're still too immature to understand how dangerous it is out there. Fortunately, I am an adult who can make choices for you. And I choose to have you stay."

The sun broke over the horizon and beamed on Wynn's ashen face. Mia's breath caught. She had seen the lord of the Lilac Kingdom only by moonlight. But in the light of the sun, his skull seemed crooked in his fur. His fangs held a yellow tint. One eye rolled ever so slightly in the wrong direction.

A coldness crept through Mia's bones. "You said I could leave. Anytime I wanted."

Wynn laughed quietly. "You can. But only if you can outrun me."

Her body went numb.

"I must go and rescent the border," he said, padding along the chasm's edge. He looked back and smiled, showing his yellow fangs. "I will give you time to get used to the idea of remaining in my kingdom."

He descended, and Mia sat in shock. Soon, great wafts of lilac scent crept up the rocks, making her eyes water and her stomach roll. She had to get Uly out of there before Wynn found him. She remembered what Uly said about his mom's clipped ear and slipped back into the vixens' quarters.

"Good morning, child," Odette said.

"Is another storm coming?" asked Mercy.

Mia's jaw clamped shut. Both vixens were missing the top of one ear.

FIVE

As Mercy and Odette went about their day, Mia snuck glances their way. One of these vixens was Uly's mom. But which one?

Their fur was different colors — elk's blood for Mercy and raspberry for Odette. But Uly's coat was darker, with blackberry tones, and a muzzle growing black with autumn. He didn't share either of their ears, noses, or eyes.

If Mia told the wrong vixen about Uly, Wynn would find out. She was sure of it.

"Come bask in the sun," Odette called to her.

"Yes, join us," said Mercy. "Before the rain returns."

Mia lay on the open rock, eyes cracked, watching the vixens for Uly's mannerisms. But they both made the same relaxed movements and spoke with the same quiet kindness.

"You look upset, child," Odette said.

"Yes," Mercy said. "What's on your mind?"

"I, um, had a nightmare last night," Mia said. "About … *ears*. How'd you lose the tops of yours?"

Mercy gave a soft smile. "No need to be frightened, dear. It won't hurt too much."

Mia's ears flattened. "What do you mean?"

Odette pricked her tipless ear proudly. "This is Wynn's way of marking us as part of his kingdom. It means we get to remain here forever."

Mia gulped. The tips of her ears started to ache.

"Don't worry," Mercy said. "He'll do it when you aren't looking, and it heals quickly."

Mia's head jerked to make sure the lord of the Lilac Kingdom wasn't sneaking up behind her. Here was another reason to figure out which vixen was Uly's mom and escape as quickly as possible; Mia wanted to get her ears far away from Mr. Scratch.

She cleared her throat. Uly had mentioned he came from the Boulder Fields.

"Where did you both live before you came here?"

"We came to Wynn as young vixens," Mercy said.

"But not before our first winter," said Odette. "You should be honored."

"I am," Mia lied.

What could she do? If neither vixen looked like Uly, and they wouldn't tell her about their ears or if they came from somewhere bouldery, then how was she supposed to tell which of them was —

Mia's whiskers perked.

"I'm hungry," she said. "Are you guys hungry?"

She headed toward the food stores. But instead of walking, she curled her front left leg into her chest and hopped.

"What happened to your paw, child?" Odette asked.

"What, this?" Mia said, looking at it. "I just stepped on a sharp rock."

"Don't let Wynn see you like that," Mercy said.

"He despises weakness," said Odette.

"I won't," Mia said, continuing to hop. "Thanks."

She'd seen exactly what she needed. At Mia's first hop, Odette's lips had curled ever so slightly. But Mercy's eyes had softened.

That night, Mia waited until Wynn was tucked in his roost and then crept from her corner and gently nuzzled Mercy's side.

The vixen awoke with a jerk, and Mia said, "Shh."

Mercy curled her lips into a soft smile. "What is it, dear?"

"I need to tell you something," Mia whispered. "Outside."

Mercy's eyes made a little upward pull toward Wynn's roost. "Whatever it is, child, surely you can say it here."

Mia glanced at Odette, sleeping in the corner. She second-guessed herself. Was Mercy trying to keep them hidden from Wynn's eyes, or was she saying there were no secrets in the Lilac Kingdom?

"Uly's here," Mia whispered. "He's hiding in the caves."

Mercy tilted her head, as if she had no idea what Mia was talking about.

"He's waiting for us to come get him," Mia whispered, "so we can all get out of here."

Mercy's smile didn't so much as twitch.

Mia kneaded her paws, feeling as if she'd just made a terrible mistake.

"Go to sleep, child," Mercy said, laying her head back down. "Go to sleep."

Mia returned to her corner. But sleep would not come until the quarters flooded with lilac scent, making her eyes droop and then fall shut.

SIX

The next morning, sunlight bled between the rocks, stirring Mia's eyelids.

All was quiet. The winds were still.

Something was wrong.

She rolled upright and found the quarters empty. No Odette. No Mercy.

Mia leapt to her paws and slipped outside. Forget waiting for the perfect moment — she was going to get Uly from the cave and leave the Lilac Kingdom right then. Even if she had to drag him by his scruff.

She rounded the chasm's edge and then stopped when she saw Mercy. The vixen was dragging Uly's freshly bloodied body up the hill. He was alive and whimpering.

Mia's heart started to pound. A snarl ignited in her throat. Would she be able to beat Mercy in a fight?

"Well, well," a voice said behind her. "Look what Mercy found."

Mia turned to find Wynn.

"Did you know about this?" he asked.

"I — I —"

"She did not," Mercy said, dropping Uly's scruff near the rocks. "I smelled him in the cave when the winds fell still."

Uly tried to push up onto his forepaw but then collapsed. His fur was slick with blood. Mia tried to meet Mercy's eye, but the vixen refused to look at her.

"What will you do with him?" Mercy asked Wynn.

"*I?*" Wynn said. "I will do nothing. I told you that it must be the mother who takes care of useless kits."

Mercy gave Uly a pitying look. "If I kill him," she asked Wynn, "will you let me return to the Boulder Fields and check on my girls?"

Teeth clenched around Mia's heart.

Wynn sneered. "I suppose the cripple's death would make up for your keeping him a secret ... Very well."

Mercy looked at Uly. "I'm sorry, my son."

Uly trembled, blinking the blood from his eyes. "Mom. *Please.* I'll be good. I'll leave and never come back. I'll —"

Mercy shook her head. "I can't spare your life and lose your sisters. Your father made me leave them when he discovered I'd betrayed him. They're all alone back at the den and still need guidance before ..." Her voice trembled and failed. "Be still now."

Uly looked so tired. Like he had given up. He squeezed his eyes shut as his mother opened her jaws around his throat.

"Stop!" Mia cried out. "You can't kill your own son!"

Mercy finally looked at her, jaw quavering.

Mia whirled on Wynn. "Why do you want Uly dead? He's not hurting anyone!"

Wynn curled his lip. "So. You did know he was hiding here."

Mia's legs started to shake. She couldn't help it.

Wynn huffed. "The runt was born deformed." He nodded toward Mercy. "This wife took pity on it and gave it some of the stronger kits' rations, without my knowledge." His voice grew quiet and dangerous. "I do not abide other male foxes in my kingdom. Especially crippled ones."

So that's why Uly had never told Mia about his past. His family had tried to get rid of him, and he was ashamed. But she couldn't think about that now. If she could just make Wynn angry, she could get him to chase her, giving Uly and his mom a chance to escape.

"Guess you're just afraid of your own son, then," Mia said to Wynn.

His smile sharpened. "You're joking."

"Nuh-uh," she said, starting to back downhill. "You're worried he'll steal all the vixens."

Wynn laughed. His paws didn't budge. "What vixen would ever den with *that*?"

"I would," Mia said, avoiding Uly's eyes.

Wynn laughed outright. "What, and have a litter of wall-eyed, wobbling kits with crooked ears and dangling tongues?"

He wasn't coming after her. She had to get meaner.

"Anything is better than you," Mia said.

"Excuse me?" The words rolled out of Wynn, gravelly and slow.

He took a step toward her, making puddles of Mia's legs, but she kept backing up.

"You heard me," she said. "Uly's a far greater fox than you'll ever be. He may be missing a foreleg, but at least he isn't missing a heart."

The sound Wynn made might have been a laugh had it not been so filled with rage. He stepped closer as Mia continued to back away.

"Also?" she said. "Your scent? It smells like shrew butts."

Wynn stopped walking. His eyes flashed upward, and he smiled. "Well, I do hope you'll grow accustomed to it in the years to come."

There was a rush from above, and then teeth were around Mia's throat, pinning her to the ground. Mia struggled, but Odette's jaws clenched tighter, making it hard to breathe.

Wynn padded close. *"Watch,"* he said, his snarling lips near Mia's. "Watch what happens to crippled kits who enter my kingdom."

Odette wrenched Mia's neck so her eyes were pointed toward Uly. He only shuddered as his mother again opened her jaws around his throat.

"Wait!" Mia said. "I'll stay!"

"Don't, Mia," Uly said pathetically.

"I will!" Mia cried to Wynn. "I'll stay here if you let Uly go! I won't put up a fight! I'll even say nice things about you!"

"Silly girl," Wynn said. "What makes you think I can't have both?"

Before Mia could even blink, Mercy seized Uly by the throat and shook him until he fell still. Then she reared back her head and hurled his body into the chasm.

Mia's blood ran cold as her friend vanished over the edge. Her ears twitched in the silence. No hiccups echoed from the bottom. No sounds at all.

Odette released Mia's throat. "There, child," she said. "Wasn't that easy?"

Wynn lunged toward Mercy, snarling. "Why did you do that?"

Mercy snarled, defiant. "So you couldn't eat him." Her eyes flashed to Mia. "Run, girl! *Run now!*"

Without thinking, Mia leapt up. Odette lunged after her, but Mia dodged around her snapping jaws and bounded clear of the rocks.

Mia ran from the Lilac Kingdom — down the hill and east, along the cliffs. Soon, she could feel Wynn's ashen breath huffing behind her, his jaws snipping at her tail. She had to lose him. Then she could find her mom — the only thing that could make Mia feel better after watching Uly's lifeless body fall into the chasm.

Wynn snapped, just missing Mia's tail. He was too quick for her. She couldn't beat him in a fight. How could she lose him when there were no places big enough for her to hide?

Mia thought of something. A trick Miss Vix had never taught.

She continued east, past the cliffs and up the scramble, to the hills where the humans dwelled. Keeping Wynn close on her tail, she pricked her ears and sniffed the air. She listened for the wet grinding of teeth, sniffed for the gray breath and the putrid black scent. If she could lead Wynn to the badger, it would fight Wynn for her.

She ran, sniffing, around the base of the hill. All she could smell was ash from the humans' fire. She turned her paws uphill. If she could just make it to the top, she'd be able to — *SNAP!*

Mia jerked to a painful stop, her muzzle thudding to the grass. Her eyes blurred on the hills, the clouds, the rain. Screams filled her ears. She realized they were coming from her. Something had caught her hind paw.

Her eyes refocused, and she saw the silver root. Its jaws had crunched her back toes, grinding her nerves together. She tried to shake it off, but her tendons rolled and grated, and she nearly passed out.

A shadow stepped to the top of the hill.

"It seems you've found yourself in quite the predicament," Wynn said, smiling. "Shame you chose not to remain in my kingdom, where it was safe."

Mia lunged at him, but her teeth missed his nose by a hairsbreadth. White pain shot through her leg, and Mia dropped to the ground, breath shuddering.

Wynn clicked his tongue. "Well, I should return." He turned back toward his kingdom but then gave Mia a pitying look. "I do hope the trappers collect you soon. I have watched the sun melt a vixen down to skin and bones, and seen the ants eat her eyes while she was still alive."

With that, his tail trailed off like smoke through the rain.

Mia let the whimpers melt out of her. She tried to shake her paw free, but the trap refused to let go. She collapsed on her side, tears mixing with the rain in her whiskers.

Uly was dead. Soon, some human would come and collect Mia's skin. And that would be that.

"Mom?" she said into the rain. "If you're coming back, now would be the time."

The storm continued to rage.

THE CLOUDS ABOVE the Antler Wood grumbled and sneered.

The little one's heart felt trapped between beats. Was Uly really dead? Was Mia going to be eaten by ants? Was Mr. Scratch going to win?

"Hey," the beta said, "when did Mal leave?"

The little one looked to where her alpha brother had been sitting. There was nothing but a pee puddle.

Two little foxes.

"You have to keep going," the beta said into the cavern. "Uly can't be dead. Can he?"

The storyteller sighed. "No fox kit is safe in the wild. No matter how sweet. No matter how brave."

The runt's ears perked. She thought she'd heard the voice in the cavern pinch a little. As if even the storyteller's heart broke at the telling.

"As for those who create the horror in this world, they have their own stories. And as to whether they feel any guilt for their deeds. Well ..."

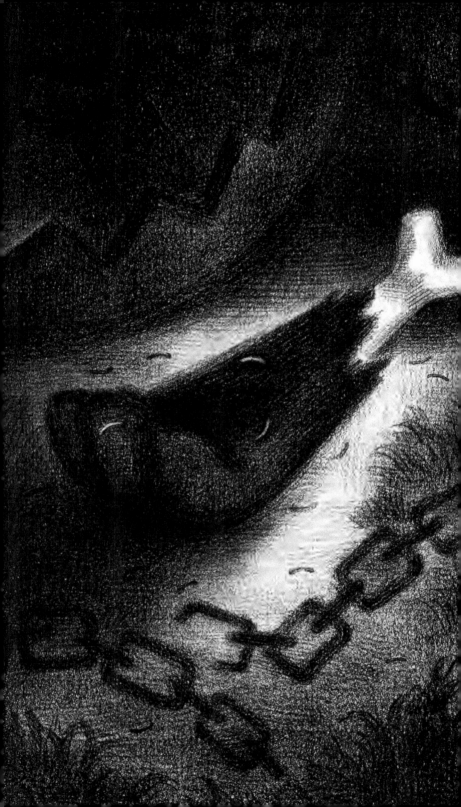

THE
PAW

THE

PAW

ONE

Mr. Scratch was pleased.

The threats to his kingdom had been taken care of — Mia, Mercy, the crippled runt. And now he could walk his rocks with pride. He admired the hill, the marshes, the scraggly branches, and the rich life he had built with his very own scent.

When he reached the chasm, he saw a tuft of fur hovering on the ledge. The fur was ashen but too soft to be his own. It must have come loose when Mercy had shaken her son by the throat.

Mr. Scratch's eye twitched when he remembered Mia's words: *Anything is better than you.*

He nudged the fur into the chasm and then continued his walk.

As the sun set, he climbed to his roost between the pillars of rock at the peak of his kingdom. There he curled up, content in knowing that the kits who'd questioned him were dead at the bottom of the chasm ... or about to die in that human trap.

Mr. Scratch fell asleep by the howl of the wolves.

That night, the scratching began.

Scrtch scrtch scrrrrrtch.

Mr. Scratch jerked out of sleep and stared woozily into the night.

"Odette?"

The scratching stopped, as if caught.

He sniffed, but smelled nothing save the cool leaf mulch at the base of the rocks. He huffed and lay his head back down.

The moment he was slipping back to sleep, it came again.

Scrtch scrtch scrrrrrtch.

He sat up with a snarl. *"Odette!"*

Scrtch scrtch.

The sound came from outside the rocky pillars surrounding his roost.

"If I have to come and stop your scratching, you'll regret it."

Scrtch scrtch scrtch.

He rounded to his paws and trotted to a space between the pillars.

There was no one there.

A moldy stench caught his nose. And he saw the thing, lying on the rock. It was a fox's paw. Its fur was gray with cobwebs. Its meat writhed with maggots.

He stepped back with disgust.

"Odette!" he howled. *"ODETTE!"*

Moments later, the vixen appeared, eyes drooping with sleep. "Yes, husband?"

"What is this foul thing doing here?" he demanded.

Odette blinked at the paw. "I ... don't know."

"Where's Mercy?" he said.

"In the vixens' quarters. She hasn't stirred."

He huffed. "Get rid of it."

Odette bowed, gathered the rotten paw in her mouth, and took it away.

Mr. Scratch returned to his roost and thought no more of it that night.

The following day, he marked his territory near the cliffs, the marshes, and the chasm so that any foxes trying to sneak in would know who they were dealing with. He checked his food stores and then he checked them again. He went to the vixens' quarters, where Odette cleaned his muzzle while Mercy kept her back to him. When the moon rose, he returned to his roost.

The paw was waiting in his bed.

"Odette!" he cried.

She appeared. "Yes, husband?"

"I thought I told you to get rid of this thing."

She blinked at the paw. "I ... I buried it in the marsh."

"Well, it seems to have *crawled back*, hasn't it?"

Odette sniffed at the paw. "I don't think it could crawl if it tried."

Mr. Scratch huffed and stared at the thing. It was small. Almost like it had belonged to a kit. A thought came to him, but he shook it away.

"And you say Mercy has not left your quarters?"

"She hasn't moved a whisker in days," Odette said. "Not since —"

Mr. Scratch growled, silencing her. He sneered at the paw. "Drop this into the chasm, where it belongs."

"Where it belongs, husband?" Odette asked.

He was about to answer, *So it can be with its owner,* but thought better of it.

Scrrrrrtch!

He whirled, ears swiveling. He thought he'd heard the scratching behind him. But that was ridiculous. The paw was right there — as dead as the kit at the bottom of the chasm.

"Go," he told Odette.

This time, he watched from the high rocks as Odette carried the moldy paw to the chasm's edge and dropped it over the side. The paw was swallowed in mist.

The next evening, Mr. Scratch hunted.

He caught a jackrabbit, but its powerful hind legs kicked him in the chest, giving him a terrible gash. He broke the thing's neck, and even though it was already dead, violently shook it between his fangs. He dragged the remains back to the high rocks, where he feasted on its liver. Then he went to his roost to clean his wound and rest for the night.

The next morning, a powerful hunger awoke him. He returned to the rabbit and nuzzled open its belly. He bit into something gray and cobwebbed and leapt back.

The paw was sticking out of the rabbit's stomach.

Mr. Scratch whirled, hackles rising, snarling toward the corners of his rocky den, searching for the intruder. But all he could smell was his own lilac scent.

Dark thoughts crept into his mind. Paws didn't just come back to life. If they did, then any number of other creatures he'd sent to the Underwood would have come crawling back to take revenge on him.

He bounded to the vixens' quarters.

"Which of you put that paw in my food?"

He realized his jaw was trembling and clamped his teeth to steady it.

Odette scrambled to her paws. "I would never, husband."

Mercy lay still. He wanted to grab her and shake her, just like he had the rabbit, until she looked at him, spoke to him. But instead he steadied his breath.

Odette had always been loyal. Even Mercy had killed her own son for him. They would never betray him. They loved him too much.

Anything is better than you.

"Shut *up*," he hissed.

Odette cowered. "I — I didn't say anything, husband."

Mr. Scratch thought a moment. "I want you to travel west," he told her. "To the chasm's end. I want you to descend to its base and make sure that my ... that that *boy's* body is still there."

"But ... ," Odette said. "But that will take days."

He stared at her.

She bowed. "I'll return as soon as I can." And she set off.

Mr. Scratch returned to his roost, where he took up the paw and carried it deep into the marshes. He dug open a swath of mud, dropped the paw inside, and covered it up. He scanned the area to see if anyone was watching. The bog was empty.

"That's the end of it, then," he said, and returned to his kingdom.

Sleep would not come for Mr. Scratch that night. The moon was too bright. The wolves were silent. His restless heart beat strange images into his head:

The corpse of a three-legged kit dragging itself out of the mouth of the Underwood, broken bones jutting out of its fur. A stir in the darkness. And Mr. Scratch's many other dead children crawling out after . . .

Scrtch scrtch scrtch.

Mr. Scratch awoke with a start. His ear spasmed, trying to determine if the sound had been real or some sleepless delirium.

Scrtch scrtch scrrrrrtch.

He leapt up and bounded toward the eastern stone. Nothing.

"Odette!"

Scrtch scrtch scrtch.

The sound came from the west now. He ran through the circle of rocks. Again, nothing.

"Mercy!"

Scrtch scrtch scrrrrrtch.

The sound came from the north.

He bolted around the circle of stones to the other side but found nothing there.

"Ha!" he said. "I buried your little paw, and now you don't have it to frighten me anymore!"

He laughed into the night, then fell quiet, listening. The stars pulsed with his heartbeat.

A shape caught his eye in the moonlight. Something was hopping across the hill.

"Odette?" he whispered.

But the shape did not come up the hill. Instead it hobbled toward the caves that wound through the core of his kingdom.

Mr. Scratch squinted. His hair prickled. The thing was too small to be Odette. Moonlight gleamed on its bloody fur. It only had three legs.

He backed away from the edge.

The scratching began again.

Scrtch scrtch.

To the west.

Scrtch scrtch scrtch.

To the north.

Scrtch scrtch scrtch scrrrrrtch.

Mr. Scratch whirled. "Come out! Face me!"

A paw crawled from behind one of the rocks. It was covered in cobwebs and maggots. It lifted and flopped, digging its claws into the earth and slowly drawing closer, closer.

Mr. Scratch's heart was beating so fast he thought it might burst. "You may have tricked my senses, but let's see you protect that three-legged creature!"

He bounded out of his roost, down the rocks to the scraggly hill. He followed the trail of blood and triple pawprints to the cave.

"I know you're in there!"

In there in there in there.

"I don't know how you survived that fall, but I promise that *this* you will not survive ..."

Survive survive survive.

Mr. Scratch gripped his claws into the soil, and he bounded inside.

A howl pierced through the darkness. *"Arooooooooooooo!"*

It echoed deep, waking the shadows with ruffles and shrieks. The cave's ceiling bled a mass of black that bent midair and came screeching toward him.

No.

The shadows consumed Mr. Scratch. Wings batted his eyes. Claws tore his nose. Fangs hissed in his ears. He could see something ahead, between the frantic bodies — two fox ears sticking out of a shallow pool.

He fought through the shrieking chaos.

He would seize that crippled kit and shake it to death, like Mercy had failed to do.

He lashed his teeth, tearing the bats from his sides.

He would kill his son, so that no one would know he could sire a kit like that.

More bats clung to his fur, tearing, biting, shrieking. He pressed through them.

The vixens of the land would respect him.

The bats sank in their teeth, ripping away tufts of fur. Of skin.

He would grow his kingdom.

Mr. Scratch stumbled, his ears deafened by a thousand shrieks.

He refused to lose a fight to his own pathetic son.

He —

Once the last of the bats had fluttered into the night sky, the stars sparkled on nothing but blood and tufts of black fur.

And Uly rose from the water with a gasp.

TWO

Three nights earlier ...

Mia gave up trying to escape.

She had shaken the trap, tried prying open its silver jaws, where her paw was scrunched, even tried biting the sliver that held the jaws together. If she could just get her teeth around it like Miss Potter's fingers had, she could get the trap to release ... But her teeth kept slipping, and the trap kept thunking to the ground, sending bolts of pain through her hind leg.

Mia whimpered, wondering how her mom had put on such a brave face when she'd been trapped. Moms must be stronger, she guessed.

Now that the rain had cleared, the high whine of insects drilled into Mia's ears. Was she cursed? It felt as if every fox kit who came near her was doomed to die.

Alfie. Marley. Bizy. Roa. She accepted that her siblings were gone now. Taken by the yellow.

But she couldn't accept that Uly was dead too. She should have listened to him and headed east across the hills. She had wanted to lead them away from the humans but instead had led them to something much worse: Uly's own father. How could a fox be so cruel to other foxes?

Mia laid her head in a puddle and closed her eyes. She waited for the humans to come.

Mia woke to a sound.

Squuuiiiiikkkkkk squirk squeeeeeee.

It was wet and squishy, and squirmed through her ears.

She turned away from it, and the trap pulled, sending another jolt through her leg and into her teeth. She whimpered and settled again.

The sound continued.

Sqrk squee sksh.

She lifted her head and found a hairy clump of moss, coiled with maggots. She was about to nip at it, to tell it to stop its squirming and let her die in peace, when she noticed the thing had claws — four thick black ones, cracked to bits. Mia was so woozy with pain it took her a few moments to see what it was.

It was a fox's paw, rotten with rain. The paw had been chewed through, and not only by maggots. Mia felt the pain in her hind paw, right at the spot where this paw was cut off. The last fox to get caught in this trap must have gnawed through his own paw to escape. And he had left a part of himself behind.

Mia sat up painfully, jangling the trap. Darkness overtook her heart as she stared at her own trapped paw. Could she do that? In order to save her own skin? With Uly dead and her mom missing ... was it even worth it?

She bit experimentally into her back ankle and yipped. She bit again, and red flashed through her eyes. She let go until the pain faded. She couldn't do it. She couldn't force her teeth to cut her own skin. She took a deep breath and attacked her foot again, shaking her head back and forth.

"I wouldn't do that if I were you," a familiar voice said.

Mia looked up, ears perked.

Uly.

Uly was there. Standing in front of her.

"It's not easy having three paws," he said. "Besides, you're gonna need all of them."

Mia blinked to make sure he was real. "I thought you were dead," she whispered, afraid that if she spoke any louder, he would vanish.

"So did I," he said. "Lucky for you, I seem to be hard to kill. I'm like my dad that way."

Mia would have laughed were she not in shock. Uly was always at his funniest whenever he came close to dying.

"I don't know if you're real or not," she said, "but if you are, help me."

Uly sniffed at the trap. "How?"

"Um," Mia said. She remembered how Miss Potter's fingers had released her mom's paw. She pointed with her muzzle. "Maybe if you hold this part down ..."

Uly pinned the jaws to the ground with his forepaw while Mia used her small front teeth to jerk and tug at the silver sliver. It wiggled loose, bit by bit, until the silver jaws shrieked and then fell open.

She stretched her hind paw, her toes, but then a sharp pain made her pull back, sucking through her teeth. She was hurt. But she was free.

She blinked at Uly. He was still there. The darkening muzzle. The sunset eyes. The scent of flower buds.

"I ... ," she said. "I'm not imagining you?"

He laughed. "I hope not."

He touched his nose to hers, and a tingling spread through her muzzle and straight to her heart, which started to beat happy again.

Mia stared at the trap on the ground, its jaws open, as harmless as a dead snake.

"What's wrong?" Uly said. "You're free."

The trap had opened so easily. If Mia had known this trick when her mom's paw was caught, then she could have saved her. She never would have gone through any of this.

"It's nothing," she said. "Don't worry about it."

Her ankle had swollen to the size of an apple. But it didn't feel like any bones were broken. She got up and tried a few steps on her injured paw.

"Ow" — step — "ow" — step — "ow!"

Uly smiled. "You're lucky I don't make you cross through a swamp or climb any hills right now."

Mia scowled and then softened. "Fair." She collapsed to her side. "How did you survive that fall? Are you invincible or something? Because that would have been good to know."

Uly smiled his lopsided smile. "My mom snuck down to the caves the night you told her I was there ..."

He'd been shivering in the pool when the whisper came.

"Uly?"

"Mom?"

He was so excited to hear her voice that he'd splashed out of the water and then had to lie flat until the bats settled again. After his mom had cleaned the mud from his fur, she gave him the squirrel she'd brought from the stores.

"Uly!" she said, staring at his stump. "Your poor little leg ..."

"It's okay, Mom!" Uly said brightly. "Now I don't have to carry it around anymore."

His mom hadn't laughed like Mia had. But she was a mom. It was her job to worry about him.

While Uly ate the squirrel, she told him how Mia had faked an injury to figure out which vixen was his mom.

"Pretty smart," Uly said.

"Yes." His mom smiled. "Pretty pretty too."

Uly just wrinkled his muzzle and swallowed more innards.

Long before the squirrel was finished and before his gurgling stomach was full, he stopped eating. He stared at the squirrel's remains. He may have had his mom back, but they weren't safe. They still needed to find a way to escape the Lilac Kingdom.

Uly remembered that Mr. Scratch had wanted Uly's mom to kill her own son.

"Aren't you still hungry?" his mom asked, nosing the squirrel closer.

"No," Uly said, stomach whining. "I mean, yes, but ... we need the blood."

He told her his plan.

They sniffed through the caves until they found an opening into the chasm with a lip of rock that jutted out into the mists, right beneath the vixens' quarters. Then, they returned to the cave's entrance, where Uly rolled around on the squirrel's remains. Mercy grabbed him by the scruff and dragged his blood-soaked body up the hill.

Mia's mouth hung open. "So you pretended to die when your mom shook you?"

"Yep," Uly said.

"And then she dropped you onto the rock sticking out into the chasm?"

"Uh-huh."

"What if she'd missed?"

"She didn't."

"Wasn't that ... terrifying?"

Uly shrugged. "Sure. But it's easier playing dead than *being* dead."

"Well, *yeah*, but ..." Mia smiled when she realized something. "You didn't even hiccup."

"No, I did," he said, laughing. "But I held it in. It *hurt*."

She snorted and shook her head in admiration. "Why were you able to do that then but not all the other times?"

"Because I knew if I hiccupped, it might get my mom killed. Or you."

Mia smiled, then stared at a puddle. She was quiet a moment. "My mom left me."

Uly perked his ears.

"When I got caught by the human, my mom ran and hid in a bush and wouldn't come out. Then she fled into the forest the moment she couldn't smell me. Like she just … gave up."

Uly hopped close. "She didn't give up," he said. "She just didn't know you were way too smart to be killed by a dumb human."

He gave her his lopsided smile. She gave one back.

"Welp!" she said, hefting herself to her paws and wincing. "What are we waiting for?" She pointed her nose northward and took a step on her swollen paw. "Ow! Ouch! It's gonna take me forever to walk."

"We can't leave yet," Uly said.

"What? Why the squip not?"

"My mom's still back in the Lilac Kingdom," he said.

"Oh. Right." Mia suddenly felt very afraid. "How are we going to get her away from Mr. Scratch?"

Uly shook his head. "I have no idea."

They sat in silence. Even with two of them, they weren't strong enough to win a fight against a full-grown fox. They were both missing a paw — at least for the time being.

"Blech," Uly said. "What's that smell?"

"Oh, that," Mia said. She looked at the moldy paw. "You don't want to know."

She continued to stare at it, head quirked. The paw was all shrunk up, almost like a kit's paw …

"I think I have an idea," she said.

THREE

Three nights later...

After the bats had flapped into the night, after there was nothing left of Mr. Scratch save blood and tufts,

after Uly hopped out of the cave and Mia and Mercy joined him from the rocks ...

the three foxes sat and cleaned themselves. Uly's mom licked the squirrel blood from his fur while Mia cleaned away the cobwebs and maggots from between her claws. On the third night of their plan, they'd made her paw look exactly like the disembodied paw that had been tossed into the chasm. Then she'd hidden behind the rocks of Mr. Scratch's roost, laid flat, and made her musty paw creep and flop toward him.

Uly stared at the pools of blood, sparkling darkly with twilight. "Is he really gone?"

"We shouldn't count on it," Mercy said. "Your father has returned from the dead before. And the bats left behind no bones."

They all fell silent, waiting to see if Mr. Scratch would reappear.

"Anyway," Mia said. "I can't believe that plan worked!"

"I can," Mercy said. "Challenge a fox's pride and he will start to lose his senses. He might even believe he sees the dead come back to life."

The winds swept in, cleaning away the lilac scent. The three looked out over the rocks, the cliff, the marsh, the hill.

"Do we stay here?" Uly said.

Mia wrinkled her muzzle.

"No," Mercy said. "This is a foul place. Wynn surrounded himself with difficult terrain — slopes and stones and badgers and wolves — so that no other foxes would challenge him. He feared if they did, he would be beaten."

"Where do we go, then?" Mia asked, gazing across the chasm toward the many paths that led north.

"That's up to you," Mercy said.

"I want to go back to the Boulder Fields," Uly said.

His mother smiled sadly. "Mia, would you give us a moment?"

"Oh!" Mia said, hopping up. "Yeah. Of course. Yes." She hobbled down the hill.

Uly's mom looked on him with shining eyes. His heart beat uncertainly. Once again, he knew what she was about to say. And he wanted to bite her whiskers to keep her from saying it.

"I thought the moment you set out alone," she said, "that you would die. That your paw would get the best of you. That something would catch you. Or you'd starve."

"I almost did die," he said. "A lot."

"Yes, but here you are." She stepped close. "I'm very proud of you, Uly."

He couldn't look at her. Instead he stared at his one forepaw, at the dark fur growing along his chest and leg. He was getting bigger. But he didn't feel any braver.

He sniffed. "I want to go home, where it's safe."

"Uly, darling," his mom said. "Home was never safe. Not for any of us."

He thought back on the stone den. The hawks. His sisters. The terrible itching. How even the nice parts came crumbling down once his father's shadow darkened their den's entrance.

"Almost nowhere is safe for a fox," his mom continued. "And yet" — she nuzzled his chin into the air — "you came to the Lilac Kingdom, the most dangerous place of all, and you made it safe. You outsmarted your father."

"But I didn't *do* anything," he said, staring at his paw again. "I only saved Mia in the forest because she told me what to do. I only swam in the swamp when she taught me how. And when we came here, I hid in the cave, too scared to come out."

"It sounds to me," his mother said, "like you acted at the exact right moment, overcoming your fear and doing what was needed to save yourself. And Mia. And me."

He looked at his mom then. At the snip in her ear. At the gray tufts in her fur. He never imagined her as someone who needed saving. She'd always been the one to protect him from the dangers of the world.

"You've been fighting so long to survive," she said, "you haven't realized you've grown up. You're too big for the Boulder Fields now. And too brave."

His mom stepped close … and seemed to shrink before Uly's eyes. She no longer stood tall above him. Their noses were the same height. His head was too high for her to lay her muzzle between his ears.

"Everything you've done has been twice as difficult," she said. "Now" — tears streamed down her cheeks — "I want you to go and live a life that's twice as sweet."

Her face wavered in his eyes. "Where will you go?"

She looked west. "I need to check on your sisters. Wynn made me leave them behind in the den, and I'm worried about them."

Uly sniffed and laughed. "I'm not. They're pretty tough."

He and his mom looked at each other. She pressed her muzzle close to his. He felt her warm fur, her breath, the flutter of her wet eyelashes. And then, long before he was ready, she pulled away.

"I can't wait to tell your sisters what you've grown into," she said.

She licked him once on the nose and then padded off into the night. He watched her grow smaller and smaller and smaller until she vanished behind a hill and did not appear again.

"You ready to get out of this place yet?" Mia called up to him.

Uly stood and sighed, taking his eyes from the horizon. "Yeah."

He hopped down the hill. "Thanks for helping me save my mom," he told Mia. "Even if it was just so I could say goodbye."

When she didn't respond, he looked at the expression on her face. Something had broken inside her. He could see it. His mom had just fought and schemed to protect him. But Mia's ...

"I'll help you look for your mom," he said. "If you want."

Mia gave him a sad smile. "That would be nice."

He nodded. "You know, Mia," he said, heart pounding, "you're better than any family."

She snorted. "You're weird."

The clouds began to break, and shafts of silvery light cut toward the ground, burning away the grays and reawakening the autumn colors.

"Are you hungry?" Uly said. "Let's go hunt something."

"How the squip are we supposed to do that?" Mia said. "You're missing a forepaw, and I can't walk on my hind paw."

"Right ... ," Uly said. "That's gonna be a problem."

The foxes trotted north, around the chasm, through the sunrise, and beyond. They came to a wide grass valley awash in greens save the two flickering foxes, one limping as badly as the other.

The first snowflakes started to fall.

"PHEW!" **THE BETA SAID**. "So Mia and Uly lived happily ever after?"

The little one's heart lifted.

"Not quite," the storyteller said from the cavern. "The story isn't finished."

The little one's heart wilted.

The Antler Wood had reached a darkness now that seemed impossible. The stars had winked out, and the moon was in hiding. The trees were deathly quiet.

"I must warn you," the storyteller said softly. "Not all kits will survive to the end."

"But" — the beta swallowed — "there are only two kits left."

The storyteller said nothing.

The beta's whiskers twitched. "I'm out of here. I'm going to pretend that was the ending so I can sleep tonight." She padded toward the den, then stopped and looked back at the little one. "You coming?"

The little one's ears flattened. She looked from her sister to the cavern and then back again. She wanted to hear the end of the story, but she didn't want to be left in the Antler Wood all alone.

"You know the way home," the beta said, and padded away, tail fading into the night.

340

One little fox.

"You've lasted a long time, little one," the storyteller said. "Longer than I expected."

This bolstered the little one's heart.

"Last chance to return to the den." Danger crept through the storyteller's voice. "Your siblings are all curled up with your mother. You could join them."

The little one whimpered. The last part of the story might not end well. The darkness might crawl in through her ears and never leave.

It wasn't too late. She could scurry out of the Antler Wood. Right then. Over the bones, beyond the cave, past the trap, beneath the branches, through the grass, across the creek, around the stone, over the log … to home.

One little fox stayed put.

"Very well." The storyteller's eyes flashed in the darkness. "Don't say I didn't warn you. One last part of the story. The scariest of them all. When Mia and Uly must learn the true meaning of sacrifice …"

THE SNOW
GHOST

The Snow
Ghost

ONE

Winter came and caressed the sky, gently laying the sun to sleep. Snowflakes wove a chill through the air and covered the valley in white. The trees lost their points, and the rocks, their edges. Ice blossoms cracked their petals across puddles and streams. And the world grew soft and sparkling against a pink horizon.

"Remember," Uly whispered, "your back paw is heavier now, because it's carrying the weight of two paws."

"No *duh*," Mia whispered back.

She crouched low, hind paw hovering off the snow. The mice had tucked themselves beneath the ice for the long sleep and could no longer be sniffed in the open air. This made hunting tricky, especially with an injured leg.

Mia pricked her ears and listened for muffled skritchings. She thought she heard something three tails away.

"Shh," she said.

Uly frowned. "I didn't say any—"

"Shh!"

She fixed her eyes on the skritching spot while lightly creeping sideways until her nose was facing northward. Purple shadows gathered in her vision. Mia wiggled her hips, preparing to launch herself in an arc, round her back, and then pierce her muzzle through the snow — just like Miss Vix had taught her.

She leapt off her front paws, and —

Her hind paw plummeted through the crust, swallowing her leg.

The skritching sound skittered away.

Mia scowled. "Don't … say … a *word*."

"Wasn't gonna," Uly said. "You, um, want some hel—"

"No."

"Okay, sheesh."

As she struggled to pull her leg free, Uly sniffed the frosty wind. He caught a faint salty scent and followed it.

Winter was the most vicious predator. Every fox knew that. Kits were supposed to spend their first autumn growing fat as pumpkins so they could survive the cold season. But Mia and Uly hadn't really had the chance. Their stomachs stuck to their ribs. Their legs were skinny as sticks. And the cold brought an ache in his stump and her hind paw that made every step painful and hunting nearly impossible. Their guard hair, thick and red and newly grown, was the only thing keeping their tails, not to mention the rest of their bodies, from freezing to icicles.

The salty scent led Uly to a trail of pawprints that ended at a disturbance in the fresh snow. Something had been hunted here. The carcass had been dragged away, but the area was spattered with blood, kept bright and red by the cold.

"Mia!" he called. "I found something!"

She shook the snow from her leg and limped over to him.

"That's it?" she said, muzzle wrinkling. "A few drops?"

He shrugged. "Beats what you caught."

She scowled.

"Sorry," he said.

He licked the red from the snow crust, and she joined him. Magpies watched from the trees, waiting to see which fox would collapse first.

Once the snow was licked clean and saltiness tingled in their bellies, Uly continued hopping through the drifts, and Mia hobbled behind him. He'd promised to help search for her mom. But after miles of traveling, they hadn't caught so much as a whiff of apple. And now the scents were all frozen up.

Still, while Mia grumbled and winter froze everything to stillness, Uly's heart continued to glow. He couldn't help it. He was never meant to have any of this. He was meant to live out his days in the stone den or perish the moment he set paw in the wide world. Every day he was out with Mia felt like learning a secret he was never supposed to know.

"Mia?"

"Yeah?"

"If we find —" He gave his muzzle a shake. "Sorry. *After* we find your mom … what will you do?"

"You mean if winter doesn't eat us for breakfast?" she said.

Uly swung around and hopped backward, facing her. "It's gonna have to catch us first."

Mia limped. "It's not gonna be much of a chase."

He swung back around, hopping beside her. His tail drooped while he searched for the right words. "Do you think you'll ever ... start a den? You know, so you don't have to keep running into new, scary things all the time? You'd just have your home and the places around it, and they'd be safe, and that'd be it?"

Mia opened her mouth to respond, and his heart flipped over. He kept talking before she could answer.

"I could get a den nearby," he said. "I could come say hi sometimes, and we could go hunting or something ..." He dared a quick look at her. "Is that anything you'd ever think about maybe doing? Maybe?"

The snow fell, reflecting in Mia's eyes.

"No," she said.

Uly stared at his forepaw. "Yeah, no. Of course not. I get it."

She must have forgotten what she'd said to his dad back in the Lilac Kingdom. About starting a den with him. Either that, or she'd never meant it.

Mia was silent a few steps. "It's just ... families can up and *die*. Just like that. Or they can leave you and never come back."

Uly watched his breath make clouds, hoping she couldn't see his disappointment. "You don't have to explain."

The sun winked out on the horizon, and the foxes looked up as clouds swept across the sky.

TWO

The blizzard lashed its frozen claws across the valley, enveloping Mia and Uly in torrents of white. Flakes whipped their eyes. Frost stung their ears. The snow piled higher and higher until they could no longer walk but had to pounce, carving a groove through the drifts.

"W-w-we h-h-h-have to f-find sh-sh-sh-shelter!" Uly called.

Mia's chattering teeth were response enough.

After a long, limping journey, they came to a dip in the land. A river ran at the bottom, rushing under a field of snow. They followed the river to a grove of pines, whose limbs hung heavy with white. They wriggled under the weighted branches and stepped onto a soft bed of dead needles. The river ran free here, save a section in the middle, which froze around the broken branches of a toppled pine, creating a snow-covered bridge.

It was warm in the grove. There was shelter around the trunks.

"This w-w-works," Uly said, jaw trembling.

Mia took one sniff at it. "No."

He tried to catch her eyes. "Why not?"

"It's just no good, that's all. It's wet and there's no sand. And something could sneak in here while we're sleeping, and just ... no."

Uly looked at her hind paw. She was more injured than he was.

He sighed. "Okay, Mia."

They scaled the roots of the collapsed pine and then crossed its snowy trunk to the opposite embankment. Steam drifted up from the dark space between the trunk and the iced-over river. And with it came a scent. It was hot and overly sweet. Like moldy fruit.

They made it across the bridge and slipped out of the pines. The open air made their eyes ache and their bones tremble. A plain of white mounds stretched to the horizon.

Uly sniffed. "I s-s-smell d-dirt."

They followed the earthen scent to an opening in one of the mounds. Its lip curled with an old root that hung with icicle teeth, piercing toward the ground.

Uly glanced at Mia. "Wh-what do you th-think?"

She blinked. There was no sandy loam. No sipping creek. Icicles were fragile and see-through and no kind of cover. But her entire body was trembling, and the only paw she could still feel throbbed with pain.

"I guess so," she said.

"Oh, thank g-goodness!" he said, bounding to the icicles. "I'm g-gonna sleep for a *w-week*!"

"Wait." Snff snff. Mia sniffed at the dark space. "There's something in there."

Uly gave her a look. "You c-can't say no t-to this place t-too. If we s-sleep outside tonight, w-we'll wake up with n-no ears or no tail or n-no *us*."

Mia sniffed again, shadows in her eyes. The smell was so familiar.

"Watch," Uly said. He stuck his snout between the icicles. "*H-hello?* Anything b-big and mean in there? No? G-great. We're coming in."

He dropped to his stomach and used his hind paws to wriggle inside. Mia crouched low and peeked under the icicles. Her eyes adjusted to the faint moonlight. Roots dangled from the ceiling. The walls glistened with frost. And there was that smell that she couldn't quite place …

"It's p-perfect!" Uly said, voice echoing. "Better than the t-trees!" He looked at Mia. "You c-coming in or not?"

Something whimpered in the darkness.

Uly jumped. Mia's eyes went wide. There, at the back of the cave, in a little grass cradle, was a litter of baby foxes. There were five of them — little balls of sandy fluff.

Mia slid the rest of the way inside. She and Uly stared at the kits in shock.

"Those are … ," she said.

"Uh-huh," he said.

"They're barely even …"

"Yeah."

"But where's their …"

Uly only shook his head.

They remained still, waiting for a mother fox to come snarling through the entrance and gather up her babies. But nothing stirred save the wind, making the icicles clink.

Tink tingl ting.

Five sets of tiny eyes shined at them. Two of the kits whined. Mia realized what she'd smelled. *Milk breath.*

Uly hopped over and gently nuzzled one of the kits closer to her siblings.

"What are you doing?" Mia hissed.

"Making sure she doesn't catch cold," Uly said, smiling at the baby girl. "Ha ha! Stick that tongue back in your mouth!"

Mia remained near the entrance, pawing anxiously.

"What mom would leave her babies like this?" Uly asked.

"Maybe she's out hunting," Mia said, eyeing the icicles.

"In this weather? When they're this young?"

Mia's heart squeezed. It was true. No mom would wander more than a few tails from her kits' den at this age. Not unless something had happened to her.

Uly slid onto his belly so the babies could nibble and lick at his face. He giggled, tail wagging. "You guys are way nicer than my sisters! *Aren't you?*"

Mia felt sick. "We should leave."

"Why?" he said, wincing as the babies chewed the ice from his whiskers.

She frowned. "Because they're not our problem, that's why."

"I'm going to pretend you didn't say that," Uly said. He made a playful yelp. "Who's biting my paw? *Is it you?*"

"Uly," Mia growled, stepping forward. "Don't get attached."

"Why not?" he said, without looking up.

"Because …" She swallowed. "Because how are we supposed to feed them when we can't even feed ourselves?"

Uly's tail stopped wagging. He hung his head. "Oh. Right."

Mia turned away, gazing into the winter night. "We'll find another shelter tomorrow. Until then … just leave them alone."

She was about to lie down and get some sleep when Uly brushed past her, hopping toward the entrance.

"Whoa, whoa, *wait*," she said. "Where are you going?"

"To catch us some food," he said. He looked back at the kits. "All of us."

"You can't do that!" Mia said. "I'm the hunter. And — and you only have three paws!"

Uly smirked. "So do you. But I'm used to it."

Mia searched his eyes. She wasn't used to him acting like this. He usually just did everything she told him to.

"The snow is frozen," she said. "Hard as stone. If you try to hunt, you'll break your muzzle."

Uly stared at his forepaw and shrugged. "I grew up with stone. I've hurt myself jumping so many times I'm pretty much *made* of stone."

"Well, what if you run into a badger out there? Or — or *Miss Potter*?"

"Miss Potter would have to be pretty desperate to walk through all this snow with no fur. And if she catches me, I'll burn her house down, just like you taught me."

Mia searched the den. "Well then, what if something sneaks in here and tries to murder the babies, and I can't protect them with my injured paw?"

Uly nosed one of the icicles hanging from the root in the entrance. "If anything tries to get in, these will break." He pushed the icicle until it fell and shattered with a *krinkt*! "If you hear that, just snarl real big, and you'll scare the intruder away."

Mia scowled. "I don't like this new Uly."

He laughed. "Well ... I do." He stared into the night, winter shining in his eyes. "I'll be back with a big juicy groundhog before ... before you can count the roots in the ceiling."

She glanced up. "Eleven."

"Um, the pebbles, then."

"One thousand and twenty-three."

He snorted. "You made that up."

She continued to scowl until he hopped up and licked her right on the nose.

"You'll be as safe as dens," he said. "And so will I."

He went to the den's mouth.

"But — but ... what am I supposed to do with *them*?" Mia asked.

Uly smiled at the kits. "Keep 'em warm."

A breeze blew through the icicles, parting the dark fur on Uly's face, making him look ... older. Ever since the snow had started to fall, his flower-bud fur had started to smell more like lilac. Though on him, it wasn't nauseating.

"Uly?" she said.

"Yeah, Mia?"

"I'm going to make you regret that lick when you get back."

He gave her his lopsided smile. "I hope you do."

With that, he slipped under the icicles and hopped into the whirling darkness.

Mia watched his awkward arcs until his tail was erased by the flurries.

"Please," she whispered. "Come back safe."

THREE

"Welp," Mia said. "Guess I'm stuck with you mewlers."

She made herself comfortable against the wall opposite the five babies, relieving the pressure on her hind paw. The wind whispered through the icicles, making the babies shiver. Mia tried to ignore them. How was she supposed to take care of kits when she'd barely had the chance to be a kit herself?

The babies kept squirming and whimpering until one of them wriggled out of the snuggle pile and hobbled over to Mia. He tried to nuzzle at her stomach.

"Stop it." She kicked him away with her good hind paw. "I don't have any milk for you."

The other kits soon followed. She pushed them away too, but then they only gnawed at her leg.

361

"Ugh."

She hefted herself up and limped to the den's entrance, where she took up a mouthful of snow. She returned, plopping it in front of the kits.

"There," she said. She limped to the other wall and slumped to her side. "Now leave me alone."

The kits chewed at the ice and then started to tremble worse than before.

"You guys have one another," Mia said, rolling over so her back was to them. "Keep yourselves warm."

Whines of desperation echoed off the den's walls. Mia folded her paws over her ears and squeezed her eyes shut. She hadn't heard sounds like this since Miss Vix had bitten her brothers and sister.

She just hoped Uly got back soon so she could talk him into leaving this place and the babies behind.

A tiny wet nose poked Mia, drawing her out of sleep.

She blinked open her eyes and found a small, fuzzy face staring up at her.

"What is it, Roa?" she said sleepily.

Her breath caught. She sat up. She saw the den, the kits, the icicle entrance. She remembered where she was.

She looked at the baby kit who'd woken her. *Roa.* She'd accidentally called him by her brother's name.

The kit sniffed at her. Mia quirked her head. He really did look like her brother. Wide face. Leaf-tip ears. Rich brown fur. A tiny black lip curled around his pink gums, giving him a permanently confused look.

She swallowed. "Hello," she said to the pup.

"Aowr-aowr-roo!" His tiny voice sputtered somewhere between a howl and a whimper.

Mia wrinkled her muzzle in amusement. "If I were to name you, which I am *not* going to do, I would call you Ro—"

The name caught in her throat. Mia's last memory of her brother was back in the Eavey Wood. She'd hidden in the hawthorn bush, watching as Roa had tried to escape their snarling teacher. She could still remember the panic in his voice: *I fail! I don't pass! I ... don't want to do this anymore!*

Mia's heart pinched. She still hadn't forgiven herself for leaving him or any of her siblings behind. If she could have just distracted their teacher with her tail, made Miss Vix chase her instead of the others, her siblings could have come north with her and her mom. And they'd all still be alive now, setting off to start their own dens.

The blizzard howled, making the icicles sing.

Tink ting.

The baby kit sniffed at Mia's face. Could she name him after her brother? Would that honor Roa's death? Or would it mean doom for this kit?

"Fine." Mia took a deep breath. "I'll call you Roa."

The newly named pup curled up by her stomach. The other kits heard their brother's contented snoozes and slowly followed, wobbling on their tiny legs, no bigger than peach stems.

First came the runt, her tiny tongue poking out of her mouth.

"Well," Mia said, feeling a squeeze in her throat, "now I have to call you Bizy, after my tongue-tied sister, don't I?"

Next came a bigger kit, whose fur was dusty and disheveled.

"And you're clearly Marley."

The fourth kit let out a seed-sized hiccup, surprising a laugh out of Mia.

"And *you*, my hiccuppy little monster," she said, nosing him close to her belly with the others, "I'll call *you* Uly. Er ... Uly *Junior*."

She smiled as the last kit crawled to join them. "And adventurous Alfie makes five."

Soon all the kits were snuggled close, shivers subsiding, eyelids drowsing, breath wheezing through their tiny nostrils. Mia sniffed at their leaf-fuzz ears, their stem-sized legs, their baby eyes, so wet and blue. She cleaned them, one by one, until their fur smelled as fresh as a dandelion field. And then she watched as, one by one, they slowly fell asleep.

Mia's heart thawed. And nearly melted.

FOUR

Bound *flumpf.*
Bound *flumpf.*
Bound *flumpf.*
Uly carved a line across the snowy mounds. With every step, the snow tugged at his foreleg, giving his shoulder a sickly bloom of pain.

Still, Uly felt good. Out of the foxes with three working paws, he was the best. He'd survived two adventures on these paws. He'd escaped the belly of the Golgathursh, *and* he had outsmarted his own father. On top of that, he'd successfully scavenged food for Mia. Sure, it was just a few drops of blood from something else's hunt. But still.

Uly felt heroic. And he realized what he'd been missing all along. He finally had someone to hunt for. And not just someone. *Someones.* There were five kits and a vixen depending on him. And that made the deep drifts and the blooms of pain and the endless snowflakes somehow manageable.

He bounded onto a frozen stretch of snow, and his ears scanned the white, hoping to catch the slightest scuffle, a panicked heartbeat, a nostril whistle. But all he could hear was the wail of the wind.

He decided to take a gamble. He widened his paws, leapt off the snow, curled his back, and drove his muzzle through the icy layer. He didn't pierce far, but he continued to dig with his forepaw until his teeth snagged something spiny. He dragged it out of the snow and then immediately spat it out.

"Great," he said, staring at the pinecone. "At least we'll have something to pick our teeth with."

Uly panted clouds. He was exhausted after just one jump. He looked back toward the den's icicle entrance, and his ears folded. A falling tree would have traveled farther than he had.

He turned his nose to the wind and sniffed the pine grove he and Mia had passed through. The snow-laden trees cast bolts of shadow across the white. Maybe some creature had had the decency to crawl beneath the branches and freeze to death. Maybe.

"The f-forest is a f-f-feast," Uly whispered to himself, and hopped toward the pines.

FIVE

Tink tingl ting.

Mia lifted her head.

She blinked at the moonlit entrance.

"Uly?"

Flurries whirled into the den.

Tink ting ting.

The icicles wobbled again and then went still.

She drew the snoozing kits closer and laid her head back down.

KRINKT!

Mia's heart leapt as the kits bounced like fuzzy crickets.

One of the icicles had shattered. It was much too thick to have snapped by itself. Something must have brushed it.

"Uly?" she said. "Is that you?"

Only the wind spoke.

She licked the babies' tiny ears until their pounding hearts settled.

"Stay put, littles," she said, hoisting herself and wincing. "I'll check it out."

The kits whimpered as Mia limped to the entrance and stuck her nose between the icicles. All she could smell was snow. She was about to turn back when something sniffed her ear.

Mia whirled, snarling, hackles growing sharp. But there was nothing there.

Her snarl faded. She scowled at the icicles and then limped back to the kits, curling around their shivery bodies. Hunger was making her imagine things. The wind couldn't sniff. It just blew in a way that sounded like sniffing. It also must have broken that icicle.

"Can everyone say, 'Hurry back, Uly'? *Aroo-roo-roo!*"

The kits mimicked her sound — *aroo-roo-roo!* — their tiny voices echoing through the den. Once she got them started, they wouldn't stop. *Aroo-roo-roo-roo-roo-roo-roo-roo!*

"Okay, okay!" she said, giggling. "That's enough. *Very* good. But enough."

Outside, the blizzard howled. How had her mom passed the long winter nights when she and her siblings were still babies?

"Ooh! Who wants to hear a scary story?"

Tink ting ting.

The wind rattled the icicles again, sending a chill up her spine.

"On second thought, who wants to hear a nice one?"

Six

Uly sniffed at the patches of dead needles in the pine grove, but he couldn't smell any prey.

Flumpf!

A sound made his ears perk. It had come from the pine-tree bridge that he and Mia had crossed. Maybe some critter had nestled between the snow and the trunk.

Uly padded to the edge of the river and got low. He wriggled his hips and then made a mighty leap onto the bridge, pouncing to pin the critter down. His forepaw struck the snow, and it shifted beneath him ...

"Oh squi—"

The snow broke, Uly fell, and suddenly, he was buried in white. Snow packed in around him, pushing into his mouth and nostrils. He paddled his paws, but the movement only made him sink deeper.

Every time he inhaled, his nostrils filled with slush. His breath grew shallow. His body went numb.

But then ... he heard something in the distance.

"Aroo-roo-roo!"

Uly stopped breathing and listened.

"Aroo-roo-roo!"

It was the kits. They were howling back in the den.

The sound spread a warmth through his body. He snorted the snow from his nostrils and tried to spiral his muzzle and shoulders. He gained a little breathing space, but the air was close and pinched and barely filled his lungs. He willed himself not to panic as he lashed his head back and forth. Soon his shoulders were free from the snow. Then his forepaw.

"Aroo-roo-roo!"

He kicked his hind paws until the snow packed beneath them and he was able to press up against it. With the last of his strength, he made a great push, and —

The snow gave out beneath him.

Uly fell through darkness before his three paws landed on something solid. He gasped with fogged relief. He was under the bridge, on top of the frozen river. The ice groaned beneath his paws, threatening to crack and spill him into the rushing water. He hopped onto the bank.

Moonlight streamed through the hole in the bridge he'd fallen through. From below, he could see that the bridge wasn't made from one toppled pine tree, but two. Uly had just happened to pounce directly onto the snowy space between the trunks and become stuck.

"Lucky me," he said.

A warm stench overpowered his nose. As his eyes adjusted to the faint light, he realized he was surrounded by dead animals. Mice and squirrels and rabbits — all killed in awful ways. Half-skinned. Throats torn out. Heads turned the wrong way. Meat left rotting on the bone.

Uly gulped. This wasn't what he'd hoped for when he'd thought of dead animals in the pines. He shuddered and left the place as quickly as he could.

He followed the ice back into the open grove where the river ran free again. He bounded up the opposite bank, then gazed back through the trees toward the den.

Every frozen inch of him wanted to return and snuggle with Mia and the kits. But he hadn't hunted anything yet. Nothing but a pinecone.

A breeze blew through the trees, pushing Uly toward the den, as if encouraging him to give up, go back. But then the breeze brought a scent. A fox's scent.

At first, he wanted to run away, hide. But then he remembered something …

Uly exited the pines and followed the scent.

SEVEN

"Guys. This is *way* too much snuggling."

With five babies pressed against her, Mia's body smoldered as hot as the kettle on Miss Potter's stove. Whenever she reached her boiling point, she would extend her paws, pushing the kits away. But then they'd start to shiver and whimper, and she would take pity on them and gather them close again.

"Ow! *Someone* keeps stepping on my hurt paw," she said, moving Marley. "Now I know how Mom felt."

Tingl tink ting.

The wind stirred the icicles again. Mia sniffed for Uly's scent, but only the cold burned her nose. He'd been gone for hours now, and the storm was getting worse.

"We need a distraction till Uly gets back," she told the kits, searching the den.

376

"I know! We'll play a game. What was that one Miss Vix taught —"

FLUMPF!

The kits squeaked as a pile of snow collapsed in the den's entrance, snuffing out the light.

"It's okay, guys," Mia told them. "Just more dumb snow."

She licked their tiny heads — Roa, Marley, Bizy, Alfie, and Uly Junior — until their shivers settled. Then she scowled at the buried entrance.

"This won't do. If Uly's going to bring us back a nice, juicy groundhog, he needs to be able to sniff us out. Otherwise, we'll look like any other mound of snow, and we'll starve. Isn't that right, my little cherubs?" She rolled her eyes. "Ugh. I'm starting to sound like Miss Potter."

She hobbled to the entrance and started to dig.

It was funny. She'd thought heading north would lead her to her mom. But instead it had led her to becoming a mom of sorts. She pawed out another swath of snow. Her mom had told Mia that if she wanted kits, they would come to her.

"Well, Mom," Mia said, "turns out they'll come if you *don't* want them too." She smirked at the shivering kits. "Only kidding, guys."

It took a while to dig out the entrance while balancing on one hind paw, but she finally broke through. Outside, the snow fell in vast sheets. A breeze brushed past her as she squinted into the blizzard, hoping to see Uly's silhouette. When he didn't appear, she limped back into the den, excited to have five tiny bodies to warm her.

"I'm b-b-back!" she managed to say through chattering teeth.

The kits whimpered in response.

"Oh, hush," she said. "I wasn't gone that long."

She counted their heads. *One, two, three, four …*

Mia's heart skipped a beat.

One, two, three, four … Someone was missing.

She heard a tiny growling and turned to find one of the kits outside the den.

"Alfie," she scolded, her heart settling. She limped back to the entrance. "How

in the squi— How did you get all the way out there?"

Alfie snarled and tugged on something in the snow. Mia reached beneath the icicles, plucked him up, limped back, and plopped him near his siblings. She quirked her head, looking at the long stretch between the entrance and the litter. With their round tummies and wobbly stem legs, it took the kits an eternity to crawl a single tail's length. Alfie couldn't have made it outside that quickly unless …

Mia's heart skipped another beat.

Unless something had carried him.

She went to the den's entrance to investigate. There were no prints in the snow. No paws crunched through the frozen layer. No wings beat the cold air. She thought she smelled the faint odor of moldy fruit. But then it was lost in a whirl of snowflakes.

She remembered that Alfie had been chewing on something, and she slid beneath the icicles. She sniffed around until she found something small and black sticking out of the white. It was a claw. She started to dig until she uncovered red fur. Four paws. A head and a tail.

Mia leapt back. It was the frozen body of a vixen. She was curled up beneath the snow, spine twisted. Mia sniffed at the body, and her heart started to settle. The fox didn't smell like apples.

Was this the kits' mom? What had killed her? Was it the same thing that had tried to take Alfie?

Mia kicked snow back over the body, covering it up. She returned to the kits — one, two, three, four … five.

"Sorry about that, littles," she said. "I just needed some fresh air."

She tucked the kits under her belly fur so she could feel the rise and fall of their little chests. Once all five were snoozing, she laid her chin on the hard earth and fixed her eyes on the entrance. She watched the snowflakes bend around the icicles, trying to get in. If something had dared to sneak into the den while she was there, then it would be back. But this time, Mia would see it coming.

She just hoped Uly made it back before that, so they could leave this place. All of them.

EIGHT

Uly pressed through the blizzard, following the fox's scent.

When he was a quarter the size he was now, he had watched his mom bury squirrels in the mud swaths of the Boulder Fields.

"Why you doin' that?" he'd asked.

"When the snows fall," she'd said, digging, "all the critters hide deep in the cracks, making them nearly impossible to catch." The hole finished, she dropped the body of a squirrel inside. "This is for winter."

He had hopped behind her as she made the caches, scattering them so they'd be more difficult for scavengers to find. She showed him how to bury the kills close to the surface so they would be able to sniff them out again once the snows came. He even helped pack the dirt down with his forepaw while she dragged twigs and leaves over the spot until Uly couldn't tell it apart from the rest of the ground. Unless he smelled it, that was.

And so Uly continued to sniff the snows for the fox scent. If this fox had marked his territory, there might be a whole winter's worth of food, buried and safe, waiting to be dug up.

Uly's nose led him to a snowless place beneath an earthen overhang. He checked to make sure he was alone and then searched the frozen mud for signs of disturbance. He found a spot that smelled of blood and dug at it with his forepaw, but he turned up nothing save roots and stones. He marked the spot so he wouldn't be tempted to dig there again, and sniffed out another.

The second spot he found had been robbed, dug up by some creature that hunted with its nose. All that was left was a mudhole, a bit of frozen fur stuck to the bottom.

A raven was perched over the third cache. Its black claws clung to a jagged rock as it tilted back its beak, choking down the feet of a muddy rodent that had been buried there. Uly hesitated. The raven was bigger than he was. He could lose an eye to its sharp bill. Or his heart.

He thought of Mia and the kits back at the den. He imagined the snows slowly freezing them to icicles, their little bones swarming with spiders and centipedes … He needed the food in that cache.

So Uly, heart pounding, lay down and closed his eyes.

A moment later, he heard a shuffling of feathers. Then the beating of wings. And finally, the hopping of clawed feet. It took all of Uly's willpower to keep his eyes closed. The moment the raven pecked at his side, Uly leapt up with such a big snarl it surprised even him.

"RRRRRAAAAAAAA!"

"Grawk!"

The raven cawed, beat its black wings, and took flight. Uly smiled proudly as it faded in the flurries. He just wished Mia had been there to see him use the nap-and-scare technique — his twist on nap-and-capture. An Uly original.

He nosed away the remaining twigs and leaves that camouflaged the cache and started to dig. The frozen mud pulled at his claws, but soon he unearthed a bright smear of blood. Without thinking, he gobbled the mouse, crunchy with ice. There was another mouse beneath that, and he gulped it down as well. He was about to devour another when he stopped himself.

One for the trip here, one for the trip back, he decided.

The rest was for Mia and the kits.

He hitched the frozen bodies in his mouth and then heard the ashen chuckle behind him.

"I would be upset that you ate the food I was about to rob ..."

Uly turned, mouth full of mice.

Mr. Scratch smiled. "But the meat on you will do just fine."

NINE

Mia stayed awake.

While the kits slept, their tiny paws twitching against her belly, she kept her tired eyes fixed on the den's icicle entrance. And she thought about her mom.

It was scary work, keeping kits safe. They were fragile, wriggly little things, so cute and tiny that you couldn't help but worry over every whisker. She imagined leading a kit, who still had her milk teeth, out of the Eavey Wood, across the open fields, and into a forest. The thought made her heart hurt. It was scary enough keeping an eye on kits in an enclosed den.

Ting ting! tink.

Snff snff.

Mia perked her ears. She widened her eyes. That wasn't the wind.

One of the kits whimpered. Then another.

"Hush," she told them.

Snowflakes whirled through the icicles, like breath through clenched teeth.

"Uly?" she said.

She listened for the familiar crunch of his paws. Watched, hoping to see him shake the snow from his coat and triumphantly drop a groundhog carcass.

"Uly," she said, more sternly, hoping to make him appear.

The snow didn't answer. Her whiskers told her something was there. But she couldn't see it. Couldn't hear it. She sniffed the crisp air — *snff snff* — and thought she smelled apples.

Her breath caught. ". . . Mom?"

She sniffed again, this time catching a faint yellow scent.

"Miss ... *Vix*?"

A swirl of snow blew into the den, sweeping the scents away. Now she smelled nothing but winter.

Mia gave her head a shake. She was exhausted. Delirious. The snow was shifting, releasing old scents. The cold was reaching into her past and drawing out memories.

"Hush, hush," she said, nuzzling the kits closer. "It was just our imaginations."

She laid her head down and let her eyes flutter shut.

Mia jerked awake. She had accidentally fallen asleep.

She sniffed the kits. Roa, Uly Junior, Alfie, Marley ...

"Bizy?" she called.

Mia was up on her paws, frantically sniffing the den for the baby girl kit.

Bizy wasn't there.

Mia darted to the entrance and slipped outside, searching frantically. There was no trace of dusty fur. No tiny-sized mews. No little tracks or flops in the snow.

"Bizy!" she cried into the storm. "Yelp if you can hear me!"

There were no whimpers. No howls.

Mia squinted through the gales crashing against each other, hoping to catch a hint of dusty fur breaking up the white. There. Twenty foxtails away, the snow bent around an animal shape.

She darted toward it and bit deep, but her teeth caught nothing but snowflakes. She whirled, sniffing. All that remained was a fleeting scent, moldy and sweet. As if the creature was nothing but a ghost. How was she supposed to fight something that wasn't even there?

The kits whined in the den, begging her to come back. Mia trembled. What was she supposed to do? She couldn't leave Bizy out there alone. She was supposed to be protecting her. Instead, she'd fallen asleep, and the baby kit had vanished, as quiet as snowfall.

Mia stood, helpless, staring into the blizzard. And she thought of her mom again. That moment when she'd let Mia down.

Finally, Mia let the tiny howls draw her back to the den. She curled up with the four remaining kits, whose whines quickly melted into whimpers. She snuggled them close as she imagined Bizy being carried through the icicles and through the snow, eyes open, tongue poking out of her mouth.

Frost crept across Mia's heart ... and it froze over.

TEN

Mr. Scratch looked more deranged than ever. His ears were chewed through, his fur shredded by bats. A gash glistened on his chest, showing bone beneath. His head sat twisted on his spine, and he angled a bloodied eye toward Uly.

"Oh, now, now," Mr. Scratch said through slashed lips. "Don't give me that look. You act as if *I'm* the villain." He limped closer. "And yet you are the one who led a badger into my territory. You made my wives lie to me. You schemed to chase me from my own kingdom. And now you're stealing the food I was going to eat."

Uly was silent, his mouth still full of mice.

Mr. Scratch grinned. "If you lay down that food and bare your throat to me, I just might let you off with one less paw. You could use your remaining two to scoot

389

back to that little vixen." He chuckled. "She might even still find you den-worthy."

Uly's mom was no longer there to help him escape. Neither was Mia. He couldn't outrun Mr. Scratch on three paws.

"Of course," Mr. Scratch continued, "if you disobey me, then I will reclaim what is rightfully mine. Your body. I'll chew you up and make a new kit that isn't a failure."

Uly's jaw trembled, and he almost dropped the mice. He thought of the six hungry mouths waiting for him back at the den. He thought of Mia. He slid onto his stomach and then rolled onto his back, baring his throat.

Mr. Scratch stepped close, his fangs hovering over Uly's throat. "Ah ah ah. You forgot to spit out the food."

Uly looked up sheepishly. Then with all his might, he drove his forepaw into his father's chest wound.

Mr. Scratch shrieked, and Uly leapt up and ran.

ELEVEN

Mia watched the den's entrance with unblinking eyes.

Bizy was out there somewhere. Cold and helpless.

The kits were quiet, pressing as close to Mia's ribs as they could manage, as if they, too, missed their sister's warmth. Mia didn't push them away this time. She just sniffed at their heads — Uly, Marley, Roa, Alfie — and regretted naming them so soon.

Her mind flashed back to that moment in the forest. The moment when Miss Potter had crouched, holding Mia out by her scruff, and Mia's mom had refused to come closer. Mia wouldn't have hesitated in that moment. If she had seen the thing that had taken Bizy, she would have ripped out its throat, even if it put Mia in danger.

Mia remembered the night in Miss Potter's house. The night Mia's tongue had hung too heavy to speak and her mom had howled outside the door. Her mom had grieved for Mia's death without even seeing with her own two eyes whether Mia was still alive or not.

Mia got up. She refused to believe Bizy was gone. Not until she saw with her own two eyes. She left the shivering kits behind and limped around the den, sniffing for clues. There was nothing but rocks and roots and frost. No fur. No blood. No droppings.

Then she remembered the frozen fox outside.

She reached beneath the icicles, grabbed its tail, and worked it out of the snow, dragging it into the den.

Mia stared at the body. "How did you die?"

She sniffed it, tail to muzzle, searching for puncture wounds. There were none. She sniffed its ears for signs of sickness. Nothing. Finally, she pawed at its muzzle, and its jaws fell open. Caught in the fox's teeth was a tuft of white fur.

When Mia was young, Miss Vix had taught her and her siblings about camouflage. *Some hunters are nearly impossible to see, because they have dirt-colored fur, or stripes that blend with the swaying grasses.*

Or, Mia thought, *white fur that blends with a snowy landscape.*

She stared into the blizzard.

If she couldn't see the thing's white fur in the snow, and the frost erased its scent, how could she track it? The kits whimpered, making Mia feel even more hopeless. If she went outside to search, the thing could slip back into the den and steal another kit.

She wouldn't let that happen.

She picked up the kits, one by one, and moved them to the entrance. Roa. Alfie. Marley. Uly Junior.

"I'm sorry, my littles," she said as they trembled in the icy gusts. "We have to get your sister back."

She left the shivering kits in the entrance and slipped back into the den's shadows, where she lay down. She closed her eyes and waited.

It didn't take long.

The air bloomed with a moldy-sweet scent.

Through the blur of her lashes, Mia saw it. The creature looked like a bit of winter had grown eyes and teeth. It walked in jerks and stops and was so skinny it resembled a fuzzy skeleton.

The thing sniffed at Mia's ear, its breath hot. Her lips wanted to curl. Her hackles wanted to rise. She kept still.

The thing padded to the pile of kits and plucked Marley up in its white jaws. Against the snowy entrance, the kit looked like he was floating. Mia could barely keep from snarling as Marley mewled and writhed in the air and then was swept beneath the icicles.

It was only then that she got up. Quick as she could, she placed the three remaining kits under their frozen mother's fur for safekeeping.

Mia set out into the night.

TWELVE

Mr. Scratch came after Uly like a storm.

Uly ran faster than he ever had, but with only three paws and a mouthful of mice, he was too slow. His father chomped his tail, nipped his thigh, and bit into his spine so hard Uly saw red.

The only reason Uly managed to stay slightly ahead of his father was that he was light on his three paws and didn't break through the frozen layer. Mr. Scratch's paws crunched through the ice, but it didn't slow him much. He bounded up and down through the snow, panting fog through his bared fangs.

Uly had to lose him. He ran along the bank of the river and then scrambled into the pine grove, his father not far behind. Uly leapt onto the bridge and over the hole he'd fallen through. Then he turned around and faced his father.

Mr. Scratch raged across the bridge, and as Uly had hoped, the snow gave out beneath him, devouring his hind legs. Uly's dad snarled and snapped before the snow shifted again and he was swallowed in white.

Uly didn't wait to catch his breath. He slipped out of the grove before his dad had a chance to recover on the frozen river below. Uly bounded across the snowy mounds, sniffed out the earthen den, and wriggled under the icicles.

He dropped the mice. "Mia?"

He panted as his eyes adjusted to the darkness.

Three kits trembled and whimpered under the fur of a dead fox.

THIRTEEN

Marley had vanished in the flurries.

Mia searched, panicking. The thing was out there somewhere — its white fur hidden in the snow. She hobbled and sniffed until she caught a faint, salty scent. She followed it to a single drop of red — bright on the snow's crust.

Marley.

She sniffed again, trying to find more of the kit's blood before the flurries covered it up. A few tails away, she found another drop. This blood was fresher, still steaming. She refused to think about what it meant. Not while she could still act. She drew a mental line from the den, through the first red drop and the second, and then she sniffed along it until she found another, then another and another ...

She saw him. Baby Marley, floating through the blizzard. Mia kept her distance, stepping carefully in case the white-furred thing heard her crunching paws and fled. It was almost too much, seeing the kit writhe in discomfort. But Mia reminded herself that because the thing was camouflaged, its scent lost in the winter freeze, this was the only way she could find Bizy.

Marley's wriggling body cut a strange path across the frozen expanse. He bobbed through the gales, floating up snowy mounds and down the other side. Finally, the kit vanished into the pine grove.

Mia hesitated outside the trees, heart shaking.

"Peaches and centipedes," she told herself, breathless. "If I go into this wood and fight this thing, Marley and Bizy will be able to taste peaches and centipedes."

She took a deep breath and then entered the grove.

The snow glowed in the darkness. Mia's ears swiveled, but all she heard was the light tap of snowflakes and the icy trickle of the river. Then something faint caught her eye. A chunk of white detached itself from the bank. It slid upriver, toward the bridge Mia and Uly had crossed. Marley whimpered in the white thing's jaws.

Mia crept to the bank, crouching behind the snow piles. The white thing hitched the baby kit deeper in its teeth and was about to slip beneath the bridge when Mia threw back her head and howled.

The thing whirled, dropping Marley on the bank. It bounded back to the drifts, where its fur was camouflaged. Mia kept an eye on the area as she leapt down the bank onto the frozen part of the river, her claws making the ice groan. She moved under the shadow of the snowy bridge.

There was Marley, quivering, tail to toes.

Mia let out a whimper of relief as she worried over his tiny head. His bones were unbroken. There were no tears in his skin. It turned out he had nothing more than a nosebleed, his poor tiny nostrils cracking in the dry winter air. She wanted nothing more than to carry him back to the den to be with his siblings. But she still had to find Bizy.

Mia set Marley in a divot on the riverbank. "Stay here."

She crept under the pine bridge, looking back to check on Marley every other step. As her eyes adjusted, she saw that the riverbank was littered with the bodies of animals — torn apart in horrific ways. She held her breath, hoping not to see Bizy's body among them.

Mia crept deeper into the darkness until her nose caught a familiar scent.

"Bizy?"

"Aowr aowr aowr."

Mia followed the whimpers to the frosted wall of the riverbank. There was Bizy. Alive. Her little tongue poking out.

Tears of relief melted the ice on Mia's cheeks. She licked the baby kit's ears.

"I'm so sorry, Bizy. Sorry I let it take you. You're safe now. You're —"

Mia gasped when she found the puncture wound in Bizy's side. The baby kit trembled as the life trickled out of her.

Mia's voice started to quake. "Shh. Mama's here now. We'll get you home, Bizy. We'll get you back. Hold on."

There came a small whine from the riverbank. Mia looked toward Marley, and her breath stopped short.

The white creature had crept up on her. It stood between her and Marley, hunched and bristling. It was a fox, with fur as white as snow. It stared at Mia through black, gooey eyes.

"I don't want to fight you," she said. "I just want to take these kits and leave."

The fox's breath rasped, as tangled as a spider's nest. Its head twitched left, then right.

Klik ... klik klik.

The sound woke the nerves in Mia's tail. She sniffed. This close, the fox's moldy-fruit scent crept up her nostrils and stirred up memories she did not want stirred.

The scent wasn't quite yellow.

It wasn't quite apples.

It was both.

Klik ... klikklik klik.

Mia studied the fox's face — his curled lip giving him a confused look ...

"Roa?"

Klikklikklik ... klik klik.

Mia barely recognized her brother. His body had been ravaged by the yellow disease. His eyes were narrowed to gooey

401

slits. His legs and tail were all chewed up, and his guard hair had grown in patches of white and gray.

"*Roa,*" Mia said, eyes burning. "It's me. It's Mia."

Roa's head jerked side to side, moving as if some invisible thing were yanking his whiskers. His jaw shivered, making the same awful clicks their teacher's had on that sweltering day. *Klik klikklikklik klik.*

"How ... ," Mia asked. "How did you survive this long?"

Something caught in Roa's throat, and his body convulsed. He was clearly in pain. Mia wanted to clean his fur, to soothe his snarling lips and gnawed limbs. But she couldn't go near him.

More tears streamed down her whiskers. "I'm so sorry, Roa. I'm sorry I left you to be chased by Miss Vix. I didn't know what else to do. I was scared."

A cold wind howled. The thing in Roa's throat cleared, and his body jerked forward, his cracked claws clicking on the ice. He snarled toward Mia in wobbles and halts. She backed up until her tail hit the embankment.

"Please, Ro," she said. "Don't do this."

If her brother's fangs broke her skin, she would catch the yellow. Her thoughts would be overwhelmed with murderous voices, and all foxes would look like food to her. Marley. Bizy. The kits in the den. Uly.

Still, her brother came, rickety, toward her.

"Okay, Roa," she said. "Okay."

Mia started to circle her brother, as if they were going to fight. But her hackles didn't rise. Her lips didn't curl. Some instinct in her brother made him circle too. With each rotation, Roa grew closer to one of the babies — first Bizy, then Marley, then Bizy.

Marley whimpered, and Roa's head jerked toward him.

"No!" Mia said, drawing her brother's gooey eyes back to her. "That's it, Ro. Just look at me."

She glanced at the half-eaten kills on the riverbank. He hadn't killed Bizy, like he had the other creatures. Was it because he'd recognized that she was a baby fox and spared her? Was her brother still in there somewhere? Beneath the white fur and the yellow stench?

"Roa?" Mia said, circling. "Can you understand me?"

Roa answered with his teeth. *Klik klikklik-klik klik.*

"Neither of us has to get hurt," she said, jaw shaking. "We can return to the Eavey Wood. You can marry Miss Vix and start an adorable little d—"

Roa lunged. But before he could bite her, a figure fell from above. Roa whirled, snarling at the newcomer. Mia saw the dark fur, sniffed the lilac scent, and for a brief moment thought it was Uly. But then she saw the wild eyes, the dripping blood …

Mr. Scratch shook the snow from his coat and looked at Mia. "I thought I smelled something familiar …"

He saw Roa and took a step back. Mia's heart was in a panic. Mr. Scratch stood between her and Marley. Roa stood between her and Bizy. She had to find a way to get the babies to safety.

"Roa," Mia said, trying to find her brother beneath the yellow scent. "Help me fight him. *Please.*"

404

Something flashed in Roa's eyes. Something beneath the goo. He stepped toward Mr. Scratch and snarled.

"This is my brother," Mia told Mr. Scratch. "He has the yellow disease. If he bites you, then you'll become even meaner and grosser than you already are."

Mr. Scratch nodded. "So it is, then."

Before Mia's brother could attack, Mr. Scratch lunged and clamped onto one of Roa's bone-thin legs, ripping it out from under him. Roa thudded onto the ice, his fangs snapping at Mr. Scratch's throat. Mr. Scratch continued to hold Roa's leg, pinning him down, keeping away from his biting muzzle. But as foam and spit flecked upward, Mr. Scratch leaned back, trying to keep it from entering his wounds. His teeth loosened around Roa's leg, and Roa lashed out, catching Mr. Scratch's eye with his teeth.

Mr. Scratch screeched. He sank his teeth into Roa's throat and shook until Mia's brother's breath came gurgled and whimpering. Mr. Scratch released him, and Roa rounded to his paws and shuffled out from under the pine bridge, his white fur vanishing into the snows.

Mr. Scratch panted, drool dripping pink from his lips. Mia snarled and raised her hackles. She could end this. But she had to be careful. Her brother had bitten the lord of the Lilac Kingdom. If Mr. Scratch's infected fangs pierced her skin, it would all be over.

Mr. Scratch saw her approaching and tried to laugh. It came out as a cough.

"Pity," he said, limping away. "And here I am in no condition to fight." He hobbled to Marley on the bank. "No, I believe I'll just take this kit and be on my way." His eyes flashed to Mia. "I don't think I need to tell you what will happen if you come anywhere near me."

Mia watched, helpless, as Mr. Scratch picked the baby up by the scruff and stepped out onto the frozen shelf of the river. If she went after them, Mr. Scratch would bite down and infect Marley. She couldn't lose another kit. Her heart couldn't take it.

But then another fox fell from above.

Uly leapt from the snowy bridge and landed right on top of his father, knocking Marley from his jaws. The impact made a crack in the river ice, and a chunk broke free, wobbling beneath them.

"No!" Mia screamed. "Uly!"

He caught her eyes, wide and panicked as the ice beneath his paws bobbed and came loose.

"Watch out for his fangs!" she cried. "He has the yellow!"

The ice drifted from the bank, and Uly, Mr. Scratch, and baby Marley were swept downriver.

FOURTEEN

The ice block rocked and tipped, spraying mist and sloshing water over their paws.

The baby lay belly-flat between Uly and Mr. Scratch. Uly tried to steady himself on his three legs, so he could grab the kit before his father could. But the ice spun and wobbled, and his forepaw kept slipping out from under him.

"Well, well," Mr. Scratch said. "Look who isn't running away anymore." He smiled his slashed lips. "If you aren't careful, you might just impress me."

Uly kept his eyes fixed on the kit. The ice block hit a rough part of the river and nearly flipped over, splashing icy water over Uly's back and stealing his breath away.

Mr. Scratch looked at the baby, soaked and whimpering in the middle of the ice. "Is *that* what you're trying to rescue? Oh, son. Have you learned nothing from your father? Let me show you what to do with needy male kits."

He lunged.

Without thinking, Uly pushed with his hind paws, sliding his chest along the ice. He managed to snag the kit and slip beneath his father's shadow before Mr. Scratch's paws touched down on the other edge of the ice. The block rocked from the impact, sliding the three foxes back and forth, threatening to spill them all into the river.

Mr. Scratch huffed. "Perhaps I haven't given you and that forepaw enough credit."

He lunged again, and Uly pulled Marley back right before his father's fangs clamped onto the fur at the tip of the kit's tail. Mr. Scratch tugged, and the poor whimpering kit stretched between the muzzles of father and son.

Uly met his father's sunset eyes. He glanced, panicked at his father's infected fangs.

"Okay, Dad," Uly said through his teeth. He released the kit. "You win."

Mr. Scratch smiled, the kit's tail hairs dangling from his teeth. "You're learning to see things my way."

"Not quite," Uly said.

He leapt, all three paws leaving the ice. Mr. Scratch's weight tipped the block, and he slid backward. Uly landed just as his father's hind legs splashed into the frigid water. Mr. Scratch gasped, and Uly snagged the kit by his tiny head, pulling him to safety.

His father tried to claw back onto the ice, eyes wide, paws scrabbling.

"Son," he said. *"Please."*

Uly scowled. "You never wanted to be my dad."

He leapt again. The block tipped, and Mr. Scratch slipped into the rushing river. He did not come up again.

Uly slid to his belly and sniffed the baby kit. "You okay, little guy?"

The kit clamped onto Uly's forepaw and wouldn't let go.

"Yeah," Uly said. "I know the feeling."

"Uuuuuuuuuulyyyyyyyyyyyyyy!"

A howl cut through the winter air. It came from the pine grove, now many tails upriver.

"Miiiiiiaaaaaaaaa!" Uly howled back.

He didn't know how to stop the whirling ice block. He could only find a red blur in the distance and watch as it shrank out of view. Mia's howls grew fainter and fainter until they faded completely.

FIFTEEN

Mia watched the river until Uly and Marley became specks in the distance.

Then she slipped under the pine bridge and curled up with Bizy — her tail protecting the baby's tail; her muzzle, the baby's muzzle. Mia soothed Bizy's shivers and cleaned the wound in her side until the baby's chest fell still and her tiny blue eyes fluttered shut. Mia held her breath, hoping to hear Bizy breathe again. But she was gone.

Mia buried her on the riverbank.

"Sometimes," she said, "there's a fire in the fields. A lot of foxes will breathe the smoke. And some of them will d—" Her voice broke, and she had to wait a moment before she could continue. "But from the ashes, the trees will grow back greener, *better* than before. And there will be lots of good things to eat. And even though the fire was scary, and even though it took some foxes away ... the other foxes will remember. They'll remember the foxes who died. They'll remember the smell of the smoke. And they'll tell all their friends and siblings and kits about it so that it never has to happen again. And all the foxes will live happily ever after." She sniffed. "Or as happy as they can be, at least."

Mia laid a paw on the little mound in the mud. "I love you, Bizy."

When she looked up, she saw two gooey eyes staring at her from the opposite bank.

"Goodbye, Roa," Mia said.

She took one last look at the river, then left the pine grove and returned to the den. There she found the three other kits — Alfie, Uly Junior, and Roa Junior — all whimpering for her warmth.

There was a pile of mice waiting for them to eat.

Sixteen

Mia passed the long winter nights by telling stories. She told the kits about the yellow stench and the six cruel sisters. She told them about the old witch of the wood and the Golgathursh of the swamp. She told them why to beware of foxes with moon-bright fangs and pretty scents. And she told them why some horrors aren't as scary as they seem.

Once her paw was feeling better, she was able to hunt again, though she never strayed too far from the den. Whenever she was outside, she kept an eye on the horizon, hoping to see a three-legged silhouette and a smaller one beside it.

Winter finally died with a howl, and the sun rose back to its rightful place. The snow melted, and the ice cracked. Streams trickled, and green sprouts crept up through the soil. The trees that edged the valley lost their winter coats. Their dripping branches almost resembled antlers ...

Once spring had come in earnest, Mia led the kits out of the den for the first time. She watched as Alfie, Uly Junior, and Roa Junior bounded through the field, trying to catch a grasshopper. The kits kept bonking heads, stumbling onto their muzzles, and chasing their own tails instead of the insect.

Mia winced, laughing. She was tempted to guide their noses, to tell them everything they were doing wrong ... but for now it was too cute.

"Mom! Mom!" Roa Junior shouted, tail wagging. He marched up to Mia and triumphantly plopped a piece of bark in front of her. "Look what I caught you!"

She sniffed at it. "Mm! This smells *delicious*!"

His little nose wrinkled. "Aren't you gonna eat it?"

"I ... ," Mia said, "am going to save it. For when you and your brothers aren't looking. A hunt this special has to be relished."

"Okay!" Roa Junior said, romping back toward his brothers. "You're welcome!"

Mia quickly pawed some dirt over the bark. Then she sighed, contented, and sniffed at their new home. The open sky. The warming grasses. The cool air whirling off an unseen creek.

It was a few hairs shy of the Eavey Wood, but it would do.

THE AUTUMN MOON sank behind the Antler Wood. The sky grew rosy with sunrise.

"Is that ... the end?" the little one asked.

"It's the end," the storyteller said.

The little one waited for something to step out from behind the trees. Miss Vix. Mr. Scratch. Miss Potter. Roa ... But as dawn seeped between the branches and birds began to sing, the thought no longer put a chill in her paws.

"What happened to Uly?" she asked.

"Why don't you ask him yourself?"

The little one whirled, expecting to see a three-legged fox hopping toward her. But the wood was empty.

Her head whipped back around. "That wasn't funny."

The storyteller sighed. "It wasn't meant to be. He was *supposed* to jump out and scare you. But ... he's late."

The little one wrinkled her nose in amusement. "Oh."

"*MI-A!*" a voice called from the edge of the wood, making the little one jump.

"COM-ING!" she called. She turned back to the storyteller. "Guess I gotta go."

The cavern was silent.

"Hello?" the little one said.

"Your name is ... Mia?" the storyteller asked.

"Yep!" the little one said, pawing at the mosses. "That's how come I stayed till the end, even though it was scary. That fox has my same name. I had to find out what happened to her."

There was a sniff in the cavern. And the little one couldn't tell if the storyteller was crying ... or smelling her fur.

"MIA!" her mom howled again. "YOU GET HOME NOW!"

"Be right there!" she called. Then, into the cavern: "I was named after my great-great-great-great-aunt, who got stolen by a human and then died. Or at least, my great-great-great-great-grandma *thought* she died."

"And who is your great-great-great-great-great-grandma?" the storyteller said.

The little one wrinkled her nose. "I never learned her name. But her front paw was all curled up like this." She lifted her paw up off the ground. "You'd think that woulda made her easier to tackle. But it didn't."

The storyteller chuckled. "Maybe you shouldn't be tackling old vixens."

The little one sighed. "Yeah, I guess not."

"And how did your great-great-great-great-great-grandmother break her paw?"

"It got caught in a trap one day. She would've died, but her daughter saved her life. That kit's name was Mia, and there's been a Mia in every litter since. That's how come I got the name I did." The little one quirked her head. "That story was about her, huh?"

"Yes," the storyteller said. "That story was about her."

"And Uly," the little one said.

"And Uly," the storyteller agreed.

"MIA! HOME THIS INSTANT OR I'LL HAVE YOUR HIDE!"

"Okay!" the little one howled back. Then, to the cavern, "Guess I gotta go for real this time or else my mom's gonna stuff me. I don't want to end up like Mr. Tod."

In the faint dawn light, the storyteller smiled. "Thank you for visiting me, Mia. Come again soon."

"I will!" she said as she romped back toward her den, paws crunching the leaves. "Thanks for the stories! Thanks for making the end good! Er, kinda good!"

"It couldn't have ended any other way," the storyteller whispered.

The old storyteller stepped out of the cavern, the morning light shining on her gray fur and the missing tip of her tail, which had never grown white. She sniffed after the little one's sweet-apple scent.

Mia smiled.

She'd been telling her and Uly's stories for years. She'd told them to the kits they'd adopted and to their kits and their kits. Mia never thought she would be lucky enough to tell the stories to kits outside of this line, let alone her mother's great-great-great-great-great-granddaughter.

"Did I miss the jump scare?" a voice said above her.

Mia looked up and found Uly, standing atop the cavern, sunlight streaming around him and the rabbit he'd hunted.

"You did," Mia said, smiling. "But that's all right. Only one kit made it to the end this time."

"I told you not to tell them about the Golgathursh," Uly said, hopping down from the cavern's top. "I *still* can't go near a puddle without getting the chills."

Mia studied his dark whiskers, slowly turning gray. She remembered the way her heart had thawed that bright summer morning when Uly and Marley returned to the den. Uly had told her the story.

Once the river had slowed, many, many miles away, he'd picked the kit up, leapt off the ice block, and swam to shore, using the technique Mia had taught him. Marley was so little and Uly so new to hunting that it had taken them months to follow the riverbank all the way back. But there they were.

When he was finished, Mia told him what had happened to Bizy, her voice shaking.

Uly had listened and then licked her ears. "If we hadn't found that den," he'd whispered, "none of the kits would have made it."

Mia had sniffed and said nothing, but she'd carried Uly's words with her ever since.

As the sun broke over the trees, Uly and Mia left the cavern and returned to their valley. They were about to slip into the dark comfort of their den when there came a terrible sound in the distance. It buzzed and whirred like a giant insect, and soon they heard the creaky tipping of a tree, which collapsed with a great smashing of branches.

The Antler Wood was changing, right before their muzzles. Veins of light were creeping through the trees. The humans were tearing down their home.

"There will be new stories soon," Uly said, staring where the tree had fallen.

Mia sighed. "And you and I won't be around to collect them."

He licked her cheek. "Or to suffer them."

The buzzing started again, and Mia sniffed. What new horrors would the future bring for tiny kits? How would she protect them if she didn't know which stories to tell?

"They'll have to learn themselves," Uly said, as if reading her thoughts. "Like we did."

She gave him a lopsided smile. He gave one back.

There came another sound — a giggling from the other side of the wood.

"Look at my tail!" the little one called to her brothers and sisters. "It's already turning white!"

"Nuh-uh! You just dipped it in bird droppings!"

"I'm not the one who left behind a pee puddle, *scaredy-paws*!"

The sound soothed Mia's whiskers.

"Come on," Uly said. "You can tell me the part of the story when I heroically tackled my dad on the ice."

She smirked. "Was that how it happened? I seem to remember you accidentally falling off the bridge."

"What? No I didn—" He caught himself. "Oh. Ha ha. Very funny."

He dragged the rabbit into their den, and Mia took one last look at the valley.

The kits of the Antler Wood knew the stories she had to tell. And while the world was changing, growing scarier with each passing moon, that thought brought some small comfort to her heart.

For the time being, at least.

SLEEP TIGHT, LITTLE FOXES.

ABOUT THE AUTHOR

Christian McKay Heidicker reads and writes and drinks tea. Between his demon-hunting cat and his fiddling, red-headed girlfriend, he feels completely protected from evil spirits. Christian is the author of *Scary Stories for Young Foxes, Cure for the Common Universe*, and *Attack of the 50 Foot Wallflower*. He lives in Salt Lake City, Utah. Visit his website at cmheidicker.com.

The employees of Thorndike Press hope you have enjoyed this Large Print book. All our Thorndike, Wheeler, and Kennebec Large Print titles are designed for easy reading, and all our books are made to last. Other Thorndike Press Large Print books are available at your library, through selected bookstores, or directly from us.

For information about titles, please call:
(800) 223-1244

or visit our website at:
http://gale.cengage.com/thorndike

To share your comments, please write:
Publisher
Thorndike Press
10 Water St., Suite 310
Waterville, ME 04901